Sweet Surprise

HONEYSUCKLE TEXAS ★ BOOK 2

CHRIS KENISTON

Indie House Publishing

Indie House Publishing

MORE BOOKS
By Chris Keniston

Honeysuckle Texas
Sweet Beginnings
Sweet Surprise
Sweet Temptation
Sweet Deal
Sweet Obsession
Sweet Tomorrows
Sweet Redemption

The Billionaire Barons of Texas
Just One Date
Just One Spark
Just One Dance
Just One Take
Just One Taste
Just One Shot
Just One Chance
Just One Mistake
Just One Family
Just One Rodeo
Just One Surprise
Just One Look

Hart Land
Heather
Lily
Violet
Iris
Hyacinth
Rose
Calytrix
Zinnia

Poppy
Picture Perfect

Farraday Country
Adam
Brooks
Connor
Declan
Ethan
Finn
Grace
Hannah
Ian
Jamison
Keeping Eileen
Loving Chloe
Morgan
Neil
Owen
Paxton
Quinn

Honeymoon Series
Honeymoon for One
Honeymoon for Three
Honeymoon for Four
Honeymoon for Five
Honeymoon for Six
Honeymoon for Seven

Aloha Romance Series:
Aloha Texas
Almost Paradise
Mai Tai Marriage
Dive Into You
Look of Love
Love by Design
Love Walks In
Shell Game
Flirting with Paradise

Surf's Up Flirts:
(Aloha Series Companions)
Shall We Dance
Love on Tap
Head Over Heels
Perfect Match
Just One Kiss
It Had to Be You
Cat's Meow

CHAPTER ONE

"So, are we getting a new sister-in-law?" En route across their father's office, Rachel paused to kiss Carson Sweet on the cheek, then collapsing into her favorite chair, finger by finger, tugged off her driving gloves.

"Not exactly." Desperation and relief tumbled about in Carson's gut.

Frozen, tugging on her last finger, Rachel stared at him. "What do you mean not exactly?"

Garret leaned forward. "I thought you said you were going to propose last night."

"I was."

"She said no?" Jillian's eyes rounded before she blew out a deep sigh.

"I never asked."

"Oh," Rachel whipped off the glove and leaned back. "So you're going to ask tonight."

Carson shook his head. He probably should have told his siblings last night the only woman so far to hold any possibilities of agreeing to a temporary marriage, had video called to announce that her troublesome ex had appeared on her doorstep with not one but two dozen roses and a diamond ring the size of Gibraltar, how could she say no.

"Sorry we're late." Like young teens with hands clasped practically skipping into the room, Preston took a seat on the leather sofa, his wife sitting beside him. Of course, still holding hands.

"How are you liking the new living arrangements?" Jillian looked up from pouring herself a cola.

"Not bad at all." Preston smiled.

"Not bad?" his wife frowned at him. "It's perfectly lovely. When Clint and your mom said they were going to make over one of the unused bunkhouses, I had visions of living like a college dorm."

Rachel smiled. "I'm guessing Mom had other ideas?"

"Yep." Sarah Sue bobbed her head. "The kitchen and table were already there, but opening up the living area by combining it with one of the bunk rooms makes the space seem so roomy."

"It's always boggled my mind how Mom can envision beauty from junk." Jillian took a sip of her drink and turned to Carson. "I'm guessing that's where you inherited it from?"

Lost in his own thoughts, it took Carson a moment to realize his sister was talking to him. "Yeah. Mom always has great ideas." Too bad she wasn't in on their plans to offer him up an idea of how to find and marry a wife quickly.

"So," Rachel crossed her legs. "What do we do now?"

"Have either of you men considered an old girlfriend? Surely there's a still single one floating around somewhere?"

Two heads moved from side to side.

Garret heaved a sigh. "What about you girls? You two were very popular in high school. No prospects on that end? Even a friend would do."

"We weren't *that* popular," Jillian huffed. "Or Blake Kirby would have taken me to the prom."

"Sure," Rachel teased, "if we were more popular he would have left spring training to go to a high school prom."

It seemed to Carson that they were all just spinning their wheels. This same conversation had been had over and over for the last few weeks. Nothing new had come from any of it.

"Maybe we should just tell Mom the truth and see if she gets on board with the plan," Garret waved at Preston and Sarah Sue, "after all, it worked out for you two, maybe that would make Mom more willing?"

"No!" multiple voices echoed in precise and adamant chorus.

Jillian leaned back in her seat and waved her glass at the youngest brother in the family. "Just because true love struck the first time out does not mean Mom would go along with us trying again. Not to mention she's a rule follower and a pretend marriage to gain access to the trust could be considered fraud."

"Not could be," Carson interjected, "is."

"She's right." Rachel pushed to her feet and crossed to the mini fridge at the bar. "Mom cannot know."

Frustrated and tired, Carson pushed to his feet. "I need to pick up an order from the feed store and then I'm meeting Chet Barker for lunch."

"Chet? You haven't seen him in years?"

"I know. His dad had a heart attach so Chet's come to see him. I think he's suffering from a guilty conscience for moving so far away."

"Hey, didn't he have a rather pretty sister you were sweet on?" Rachel's brows curled into a deep V.

Carson shrugged. He wasn't exactly sweet on Carolyn Barker, but she was awfully easy on the eyes and her sense of humor could easily turn a bad day around. "I thought I'd catch up on how Carolyn's doing. Maybe that could be an option."

"Now you're talking." Jillian smiled. "Second chance at romance could work with Mom."

Again, Carson shrugged. All the siblings had come to understand that unlike Sarah Sue who agreed to marry Preston for the family, any woman—or man—who agreed to be wed for a year was going to need at least some financial compensation. Maybe if he was lucky, Carolyn was not only single, but looking for an easy way to earn a down payment on a condo somewhere.

This couldn't be happening. Jessica Pratt sat across from the doctor's desk, waiting impatiently for the bad news. Ever since her ex had showed up drunk as a skunk, pounding on her door at the stroke of midnight, her world had turned even more upside down than it had been since Todd walked out on his family, cleaning out their bank accounts on the way to the divorce lawyer. She'd not wanted to let him in, but when he broke down crying on the other side of her door, muttering he was sick, how could she not let him in.

Four cups of coffee later, she'd learned just how sick. Todd Pratt had Huntington's disease. His dad had died at a young age from the disease, but he and his mother had hoped that showing no signs of the disease by the same age, Todd would not have inherited the dreadful gene. Apparently, hope wasn't worth much.

It had taken her hours after he left to finally give up on getting any sleep. While she wanted nothing to do with the good-for-little ex-husband, he had given her a precious boy, and would need someone to look after him. His mother was young and had been through this once, and his sister was available to help, but she couldn't shake the guilt that despite his character flaws, she should be there for him.

Of course, she didn't get far with that mindset when she began to worry about her own son. What if Colton had inherited the same ugly disease? The thought of her little boy someday having his life cut horribly short by such a miserable disease had her crying into her pillow for hours.

For the next few weeks, she went through the motions of day-to-day living, in the back of her mind debating what to do next. After finding herself more and more unsettled with each passing day, she decided she was not the kind of person who could go through life just waiting for a genetic mutation to strike. Knowing if Colton had the disease was better than waiting for the other shoe to fall.

Which brought her full circle to today. She'd found a specialist who agreed to do the testing on Colton. A simple process that she'd had to run up her credit card for, but it had to be done. The not knowing was eating away at her. The only challenge now was the phone call from the nurse. She could still hear the soft-spoken woman's voice replaying in her head.

"Mrs. Pratt? Dr. Sullivan would like to discuss your son's test results in person. When would you be available to come in?"

In person. What awful fate awaited Colton that Dr. Sullivan couldn't simply say, yes or no? Then her mind ran around with every worse case scenario from Colton was already showing symptoms she hadn't noticed, to they found cancer somewhere, or some other deadly disease was found in his genetic makeup. It hadn't helped her nerves any that it had taken four weeks to get the initial consultation with Dr. Sullivan and now he was willing to squeeze her in anytime rather than wait.

Not able to stand another minute with her terrified imagination, she'd taken the afternoon off of work and hurried to the Doctor's office. Two hours later she'd been moved from the lobby to his office, but was still waiting. In her lap, the confetti of tissue paper she'd methodically twisted and tugged, was the only visible sign of just how scared she was.

"Sorry for the delay, Mrs. Pratt."

"I appreciate you squeezing me in like this."

"Yes." An older man with salt and pepper hair and just enough padding to be considered jolly, slid into his seat and opened a folder. Perusing through several pages, he pulled out a sheet and setting it in front of him, steepled his fingers. "I recently diagnosed your husband—"

"Ex-husband," she interrupted.

"Yes. Ex-husband who has Huntington's."

She bobbed her head willing herself to stop shredding what was left of the tissue in her hand.

"First of all, I am very happy to tell you that your son does not have any sign of inheriting the diseased gene from your husband."

A thousand-pound anvil slid away from her shoulders. "That's wonderful news." Except the doctor wasn't smiling. "What else is wrong?"

The doctor picked up the paper in front of him. "Because I am your ex-husband's physician, he agreed to have the same DNA testing done as we performed on your son."

Again, her head nodded slowly.

"I don't mean to be indiscreet, but are you aware that Colton is not your ex's biological son?"

What? Not Todd's son? But…

"I'm guessing by that deer in the headlight expression, the answer is no?"

She bobbed her head. The only reason she'd married Todd was when she'd learned she was pregnant.

"You may want to reach out to whoever else could be his father."

This time she could only blink. Whoever else. She'd only slept with one other man the entire time she and Todd were dating. One time. One Man. Holy Mary, mother of Jesus, Carson Sweet was Colton's father.

CHAPTER TWO

As much as he hated to admit it, he'd taken to eating lunch at the café every day this week. The stress of not finding a willing female to help save the ranch was making it harder and harder to look his siblings—and mother—in the eyes. He had no idea why, but he felt as the second born it was his responsibility to move forward, more than garret or the girls.

Of course Kade, would be the most logical as the oldest, but away serving his country meant passing the baton to Carson. Removing his hat, he hung it on a hook by the booth and slid in. No standing on ceremony at the café. If there was an open table, the locals took it.

Agnes walked past him. "Be back in just a moment."

Nodding, he glanced up at the recent addition of a blackboard with chalk specials on it. For years, the menu had never changed, but for some reason, Agnes decided it was time for a little variety. Glancing at the booth in front of him, he noticed a little boy sitting by himself. Studying the child, he didn't recognize the face. Honeysuckle wasn't so small that he knew ever single resident, but it was small enough that he knew most. Often he could figure out who the parents were just by looking at the offspring's face. There were usually only two choices, looks like their mother or father. Every once in a while a grandparent made the connection, but this time he was stumped.

Lifting his gaze from his artwork, the little boy smiled at him. No fear of strangers. Carson supposed in a small town like this that was a good thing. A moment later the boy looked up again, this time not fully raising his head, just glancing Carson's way through thick lashes. The kid had the most startling green eyes. Not since, well, not for a long time had he seen eyes quite so green.

Wondering what was taking his parents so long to return to the table, Carson slid out from the booth and taking a few steps, slid into the empty seat in front of the boy. "Mind if I join you?"

The little boy shook his head.

"My name is Carson Sweet."

"That's a funny name." The boy frowned.

Carson chuckled. He didn't have much experience with little kids, but the boy was right, the family name was the butt of many a joke during his childhood. "What's your name?"

"Colton." The little boy didn't look up.

"What are you drawing there?"

"A robobird."

"Robin bird?"

"No. Robobird. A robotic bird."

This kid must be older than he looked. "How old are you?"

"Nine." He continued coloring.

Had Carson had that much imagination at nine? I remembered playing cops and robbers with his brothers, helping his dad, or at least their dad let them think they were helping, to build a tree house, but he had no memory of being even a little creative in his stick figure art work. "It's a nice picture."

The kid looked up and grinned. His smile was wide and bright and reminded Carson of his mother's smile. One that he and his brother Garret had inherited. If Colton learned how to use that classic grin as he grew, the world could be his on a silver platter.

"Where are your folks?" Carson reached over and picked up a brown pencil, then straightened out a paper napkin and began doodling.

"My Dad is sick. He says he's dying, but my Mom went to the bathroom." Those big green eyes looked up at him. "Is my Mom going to die too? She's been really weird lately."

The sudden sadness that filled the young artist's eyes,

squeezed at Carson's heart. What the hell was he supposed to say to the kid?

"Hey, that's good." The little boy's eyes lit up as he reached for Carson's napkin. "It's a house."

Carson bobbed his head.

"Cool."

For a while, Carson had tinkered with the idea of becoming an architect. Like Colton, he loved to draw, but eventually he settled on a standard business degree and then found himself flipping houses. Only on the most complicated of projects did he have to pay an architect or engineer to submit professional drawings to the city for permits, but almost always the drawings were merely renderings of the work he'd given the professionals.

"That's pretty cool too." The kid had lots of talent. The drawing was clearly a bird, a red bird, but with sleek lines and shadows highlighting the metal structure verses ordinary feathers. Somehow, Carson suspected if the kid wanted to draw a real bird with feathers, he'd probably do a great job.

"Excuse me," A harsh female voice sounded over his shoulder. "What are you doing with my son?"

"Sorry, ma'am." Putting down the pencil, he slid out of the booth, drawing to his full height. "I meant no harm the boy…" When his gaze leveled with the same brilliant green eyes that Colton had, Carson almost swallowed his tongue. "Jess?"

For the better part of a week, Jess had debated how to tell Carson that he had a son. Finding him online had been easy. How could anyone forget a town with a name like Honeysuckle? The problem was that she couldn't bring herself to tell him this kind of news over the phone or an email. Instead she'd spent the entire drive from Dallas playing over what she would say, and she nixed every scenario.

Once they'd hit Honeysuckle, her stomach was so tied in knots, she was convinced she was going to throw up if she didn't get some cool water on her face. Now, what to do or say wasn't coming any easier than it had in the car. "Hi." She almost rolled her eyes at herself, how lame was that… hi.

"Uh," Carson took a step back. "He's a nice boy. Lots of talent."

"Lord knows where he got it. I can't draw a stick figure to save my life." Though spotting the napkin on the table, she remembered that whenever Carson was bored in class, he'd doodle the most amazing designs. Closing her eyes, not that she'd had any doubts after sitting down with the doctor, but right about now, a lot of missing pieces were falling into place. Colton's artistic talent, the brilliant smile that didn't mimic his mother or father…er, Todd. His eyes were so much like hers that she never questioned his kinship to Todd. How stupid had she been?

"Are you all right?" His gaze narrowed under dark brows that she remembered all too well.

"Sorry. I was just thinking."

"Maybe you should sit. You're looking a little green around the gills."

Sitting sounded good. She slid in next to Colton and gestured for Carson to retake his seat. "Join us please."

From where she sat, it looked like he swallowed hard before finally nodding and sliding back into the booth. "So, what brings you to this part of the country?"

Oh heavens, wasn't that a loaded question. She certainly couldn't spit it out in front of Colton. "It's a bit complicated."

All he did was drop his chin in a short nod.

"So. I see you've made a new friend." Agnes stopped at the table. "Do we know what we want?"

"Oh." Carson glanced at Jess and then Colton before returning his gaze to Jess. "I didn't mean to intrude."

"You're not intruding." They had to start somewhere, didn't they? "Are you meeting someone?"

He shook his head.

"Then we'd love to have you join us."

They each placed an order and then sat in very uncomfortable silence. She needed to say something to alert him, but what? How? And more importantly—where? It had been almost an impulse to get in her car and start driving across Texas. A couple of times she came within inches of turning around, but what to? Her job had been downsized, without child support from Todd, she couldn't afford the rent on the house. Perhaps once Carson learned that Colton was his son, maybe then he would contribute financially so she could keep a roof over their heads.

Unless, of course, he's mad as hell and wants nothing to do with her or her son after what must look like a massive betrayal.

"Where do you live now?" His gaze was on Colton, but the question was obviously directed at her.

"Dallas." They'd both attended University of Texas in Austin and then once she and Todd married, he'd moved her as far away from her friends as he could take her. She supposed she was fortunate he didn't take work in Alaska.

Carson bobbed his head. "He's really talented."

Having moved on to another picture, Colton was happily drawing some kind of flying dinosaur. She could never remember the names of the different ones, but Colton knew them all. A grin tugged at the corners of her mouth, she was so proud of Colton, and well adjusted he seemed despite having a disinterested father.

Her gaze drifted to Carson. In just a few minutes, he'd paid more attention and more compliments to her son than Todd had in the first few years of Colton's life.

The waitress with the name tag Agnes reappeared with all the dishes stacked up her arm. Jess had tried that once, every single dish came crashing down on the dining hall floor and she never tried it again.

"I'll be back with your drinks." Another few moments and Agnes did indeed reappear with a tray of drinks. The woman had barely set them down in front of everyone when Colton had nearly devoured more than half his hamburger.

"Careful, buddy. You need to chew." There was no

reproof in Carson's voice, only a hint of amusement. Shaking his head, he leveled his gaze with hers. "I was the same way growing up. Shoved food in my face as if I were never going to be fed again. Drove my mother crazy."

Like she'd said, so many pieces were starting to fall into place. Todd would scold Colton unmercifully, telling their son… her son, that he wasn't a barbarian or a wild animal.

"May I be excused? I need to use the restroom." Colton wiped his mouth with the napkin and then shifted to face his mother.

She nodded. "It's across the café, through that hallway, last door on your left."

Rolling his eyes, he shook his head. "Mom, I'm not five anymore. I can find the bathroom on my own."

"Yes, dear." She couldn't help but smile. Were they supposed to grow up at only nine?

A wide grin had sprouted on Carson's face. "I still have conversations like that with my mother."

"How to find the bathroom," she teased.

"On being grown up."

Her gaze remained on Colton's back until he disappeared down the rear hallway. "You have no idea how hard it is for me to let him do that on his own. The world is filled with so many crazy people."

Carson nodded. "That's thankfully not a problem we tend to have in small towns."

"No," she sighed. "I suppose not."

"So why don't you tell me what's so complicated to bring you to Honeysuckle?"

She sucked in a fortifying breath. "You."

His dark brows rode high on his forehead and those deep blue eyes that had practically hypnotized her from the first day of class, seemed to be seeing right through her.

"Okay. While I'd like to carefully pull this Band-Aid off, just ripping it quickly is the best way."

His head nodded, but he didn't say a word.

"The reason I quit school and ran off to marry Todd is because I was pregnant with Colton."

Again his head bobbed and he muttered, "Makes sense."

"Except for one major flaw in my plan."

Only one brow rose high with curiosity.

"Todd was an idiot, he didn't grow up, didn't mature, and fatherhood did not make him a better man. Of course the bigger problem now is that Todd's been diagnosed with Huntington's disease."

Carson closed his eyes momentarily. "That's why your son said his father is dying."

"Eventually, yes." She sucked in another deep breath. "But in having Colton tested for the gene that causes the disease, I learned something surprising. Actually, shocking would be a better word."

Leaning forward, Carson's eyes filled with concern. "He already has it?"

She shook her head. Here goes the Band-Aid. One fast tug. "Todd isn't Colton's father. You are."

CHAPTER THREE

Stunned didn't begin to describe the multitude of emotions running through Carson's system at the moment. Everything from scared, to angry, to confused, to downright flabbergasted winning out on the top of the emotional ladder. "How?"

Her eyes widened and he shook his head.

"I understand how the birds and the bees work, what I don't understand is how didn't you know?"

"I've been asking myself the same thing ever since finding out. It honestly never occurred to me that one night could possibly have been the cause of my pregnancy. Todd and I had dated for most of the school year. Logic told me he was the father."

Logic. Feeling his hands clench at his sides into tight fists, he stretched his fingers and forced a deep breath. About to open his mouth with a string of questions popping into his head, Colton reappeared at the table, sidling up to his mother, returning to his artwork.

For the next little bit, they finished their meals, though to Carson every bite tasted like sawdust. He had zero desire to eat, but he also had zero desire to alarm Colton. Could it be possible that paternal instincts would kick in so quickly? Didn't they need time to grow?

"Do you design houses for real?" Colton asked without looking up.

"Sort of. I buy and sell houses and usually that means some simple drawings to show the contractors what I want them to do."

"Cool." Raising his head to meet Carson's gaze, a smile spread across the young boy's face. "I think it would be way cool to see your drawings come to life."

That made Carson smile. "Yes. Way cool." Maybe if circumstances permitted, Carson could show his son some of his before and after photos along with his drawings. His son. *Son.* Suddenly his heart lurched in his chest and threatened to lodge in his throat. A son with the only woman he could never quite forget. Through the years he told himself that like the old 70s song, he probably remembered her more fondly than reality was. Except, he hadn't forgotten how beautiful she was, and the sweet smile on her face and sheer pride and joy reflected in her eyes as she watched her son return to his drawings, told Carson she was definitely the kindhearted person he remembered.

When Agnes showed up with the bill, he and Jess both reached for the check. Shaking his head, he fought off the tingling sensation shooting up his arm, and stared her in the eyes. "This one is on me."

Was that relief he saw cloak her expression. "Thank you."

Yep. She was tight on money. Made sense raising a young boy. Especially one who ate every single crumb from his plate. "I guess with your husband so sick, working is tough?"

She scoffed at his comment. "He didn't need to be sick to not work, and for the record, he's my ex-husband."

Ex? "How long have you been divorced?"

"Less than a year. I tried to make it work, really I did. I thought it was best for Colton if I stuck it out, but then one day I saw the crushed look on Colton's face when Todd told him to stop with the stupid drawings and grow up. I'm sure it wasn't the first time I'd seen that much hurt in his eyes, but it was the first time I realized that no father at all was better than a bad one. Of course, getting sick gave Todd a legitimate excuse not to keep up with his child support checks, and then, when the DNA tests came through, Todd wanted nothing to do with either of us."

That made little sense to Carson. He had lots of friends who'd married someone with children and they loved those kids as much as their own. Then again, Carson always thought Todd was an arrogant, conceited guy who most Texans would describe as all hat and no cattle. A part of him wished he hadn't been right, then again, if Todd had turned into a good husband and father, Carson wouldn't know he had a son.

Agnes returned with the change from their lunch and Carson scrambled for what to do next. Right now, he needed to think, but there wasn't enough time for that. "Want to go for a walk?"

Colton's head snapped up and his eyes brightened. "Can we go to the park? I saw corn hole courts."

"You like corn hole?" Somehow that made Carson want to smile.

The fire left his eyes. "I used to, but I haven't played in a long time."

"Then corn hole it is." Carson pushed to his feet and waved Jess and Colton ahead.

Walking down main street, Carson pointed out the candle shop. "This belongs to my sister Jillian. When she said she wanted to open a candle shop, we thought she was completely insane. Turns out she knew more than any of us."

"I love candles," Jess smiled at the candles in the window.

A couple of storefronts away, he pointed to corn hole heaven. "My mother's two sisters own this store. Honeysuckle is the corn hole capital of Texas."

"Really?" Colton seemed to study each item in the window.

The kid was taking it all in. Every window, every shop, his eyes seemed to be filled with the same wonder as a kid on Christmas morning. Not any kid, his son. How the heck did his world change on a dime? The same way all their fates had shifted the day they found their mother snagged on the fence. Life was always full of surprises, though this surprise was a doozy.

As soon as the park came within view, Colton practically danced in place. "Can I run ahead?"

Carson could see the hesitancy in Jess's eyes. Not sure

what his place was in this particular situation, he nudged her arm gently and when she turned to him, he gave a slight nod of his head.

"Go on," Jess smiled at her son, "we'll be right behind you."

He'd taken two more steps when it suddenly struck him that fate may have just put the answer to everyone's problems right in his lap.

Throughout the years since leaving college, she'd often thought of Carson, of how her life might have been different if she hadn't found out she was pregnant and married Todd. She and Carson had sat beside each other for two semesters of statistics and then again for micro and macro economics. They'd been friendly. Somehow when she was stressing the most about a test or project, he'd make her laugh, or at least smile. Eventually they'd gone from classmates to friends. They'd gone out to lunch or dinner a few times, usually with a crowd of friends; her favorite pastime had been bowling. Todd always joined them for that. She remembered how Todd always tried to show up Carson, but Carson always beat him. One man tried so hard to be a big shot and the other simply was.

She'd finally figured it out one night at a frat party. Todd had drank way too much, he was making a total fool of himself, and when she tried to get him away from the party he'd gotten really loud and obnoxious. Called her every name in the book. Carson walked in just as Todd had shouted to her that she wasn't good enough for him, would never be good enough for him. Todd lifted his hand as if he were going to strike her, when Carson grabbed it, twisted it behind his back, and without saying a word, shoved Todd forward and didn't stop until he'd pushed Todd out the front door. When she'd started to run after him, Carson stood in front of her, leveled his gaze with hers, and softly said, "You're worthy of a king, not a drunk."

They'd spent the rest of the night together, had a few drinks, and somehow the night got away from them, in more ways than one. The next day, she'd decided she was done with Todd, and that she wanted to see where things with Carson could go. That lasted for all of two weeks. They'd taken it slow, done more things without large groups of friends and fellow students, and then, then she'd taken that pregnancy test and everything changed.

"Will you be staying long?"

She heard his voice, but her mind was still in Austin almost ten years ago. "I'm sorry. What did you say?"

"How long will you be staying in Honeysuckle?"

Good question. "I haven't really thought it through. Coming was a bit of an impulse."

Carson chuckled. "That sounds like the Jessica I knew and, well, knew."

There was no way she could afford a good hotel, but maybe a bed and breakfast. Maybe stay a few days. "Is there a hotel in town?"

"A very nice one. There's also a motel on the northern outskirts of town."

She nodded. "Is there a bed and breakfast in town?"

"Several."

"Mom," Colton came running up to them. "Some kids asked me to play with them. Can I?"

"I don't know. Can you?"

"Mom." Colton rolled his eyes the way only a ten year old could. "May I?"

As usual, her son made her smile, oddly enough, just like his father, his real father. "Yes, go on."

Carson had stopped walking and was staring after her son. "Does he have a lot of friends in Dallas?"

"Not really. Dallas isn't a small town." She didn't want to say that there weren't a lot of kids she'd feel comfortable letting him play with in their neighborhood. Well, it wasn't really the kids but their families. It was better Colton played inside.

"No. I can't imagine having grown up anywhere but here."

All she'd seen of the town and the people in the last couple of hours was the main street, the café, and a few shop windows, but already she understood what he meant.

"Listen." Carson stopped and turned to look at her. "I don't mean to be forward, but there's room at the ranch for you and Colton."

"I can't impose on your family like that."

He shook his head and smiled. "It's not an imposition and technically, they're Colton's family too."

"I don't know." Looking to where Colton was laughing and playing with the other kids, she needed to be smart. "I bet he'd like seeing a real ranch."

"Then it's settled. I'll just call ahead and tell Mom to expect company." His gaze drifted off to where Colton had just landed a hole in one and was cheering as if he'd won the Irish Sweepstakes. "My mother will be over the moon."

"Will she?"

His head snapped around to face her again. "I gather Todd's mother wasn't over the moon with her grandson."

She shrugged. "You have to figure anyone who raised Todd wouldn't be much better with a grandson. She wanted a girl. Behaved as if it was my fault I gave birth to a boy. So, no, she wasn't over the moon. She was actually overjoyed to learn that Colton wasn't her son's child. You might say, they both washed their hands of us."

Carson frowned. "Does Colton know?"

"That his father wants nothing to do with him?" She shook her head. "Todd didn't have much to do with Colton when we were married. Even less since the divorce."

"Listen," he slowly reached for her hand. "There's a lot to work out, but I promise you, everything will be all right from now on."

Oh she really hoped so. Not for her, but for her son. Maybe, just maybe, now Colton would have the life she'd always wanted her son to have.

CHAPTER FOUR

For the short ride to the ranch from town, Carson spent more time watching the car in his review mirror than the road. His mind played pictures of Colton drawing, eating, smiling, and playing the park over and over on a never-ending loop. Thrown in for good measures were visions of what he might have missed. Colton's first steps, first words, first drawing pinned to the fridge with a magnet—probably holding a school picture. All the things he'd missed. Things he could not recoup. His head felt ready to explode.

Never had so many tumultuous emotions battered him at once. Joy at a son, shock at a son, sorrow at all he'd lost with that son. And Jess. The woman who'd gotten under his skin so many years ago and never quite worked her way out was back. Maybe back wasn't the right word, but she was here, and she was no longer married, and now they shared a son.

What he needed to focus on now, wasn't how he felt or didn't feel, but how much should—or could—he tell his mother about Jess and Colton. He had called ahead and told his mom that an old college friend was in town and they'd be staying at the ranch. His mom had been so freaked at having to straighten up and prepare two rooms for their unexpected guests in the time it took to drive from town, that she barely asked any questions, rushing off to get the house ready. Where for most people tidying up means picking up a few misplaced items and maybe tossing dirty dishes in the sink or dishwasher, he suspected his mother, on the other hand, would be on all fours scrubbing bathrooms and mopping floors.

Turning under the gate, he glanced at the rear-view mirror for the umpteenth time. So much to figure out. So much to deal with. And yet, all that was now rattling around in his brain was if Jess showing up in his life again was a gift from God or a cruel trick from hell.

By the time he parked his car in front of the house and stood by the driver-side door, waiting for Jess to park beside him, his mother and sisters were on the front porch. The only one smiling was his mother. Most likely, that had something to do with his having ignored the texts and calls from both Jillian and Rachel. He knew they'd have more questions than he'd have answers for.

If Jess thought she was nervous over arriving in town and after all these years seeing Carson again, the prospect of meeting his entire family wasn't much better. She'd been taking deep breaths for the last ten minutes and considered simply turning around and finding any lodging, anywhere but here. Then she'd remind herself of the stack of bills she'd been playing *borrow from Peter to pay Paul* with, and free lodging was hard to turn down.

The sight before her wasn't helping. Coming to a stop in front of the massive house, half old-fashioned logs, half massive stone, the place looked like a cross between the Ponderosa from the old western television show she'd watch in reruns with her grandmother, and an old Scottish castle or university. If his mother and two of his sisters weren't on the porch watching them intently, she'd take a few minutes to just sit and stare at the beautiful house. Once she parked beside Carson, he circled around the back to her door and managed to tug it open before she could exit the car on her own.

The gesture made her smile. He'd always been so good at opening doors, pulling out chairs, and helping her on with jackets and sweaters. "Still the gentleman."

He didn't say a word, but took her hand and waited for

Colton to exit the car and come to stand beside them. "Told you my mom would be delighted with company."

His mother was indeed sporting a smile as wide as the Rio Grande, but the other two women at either side of her didn't look as enthused about the prospect of two strangers for houseguests.

As if able to read her mind, Carson leaned in and whispered for her ears only. "They're going to love you, both of you. I promise."

And just like that his mother flew off the porch and drew her into a stuffing squeezing embrace. By the time Mrs. Sweet had let her go, the other two women who seemed less than content only moments ago, had transformed into smiling, gracious, and welcoming people. Could she have imagined the sour faces?

"Come on in and we'll get you settled. You'll be using my old room, and your son will stay in Kade's room. He's my oldest boy."

"The one in the military?" she was surprised she remembered.

His mother's already pleasant expression brightened even more. "You know Kade?"

"Back in school Carson might have mentioned him a time or two thousand."

His mother looked over her shoulder and grinning at Carson, sheer joy and pride shone in her eyes. "They were always close."

The next thing Jess knew, her small bag was unpacked and her clothes put away in a spacious room that somehow still felt cozy with lovely views of the expansive ranch that seemed to roll out before her like a massive carpet of green with distant speckles on the horizon that she suspected up close would be rather large cattle.

"Mommy." Sitting on the bed, his attention split between watching his mother unpack and sketching a new drawing, Colton glanced up at her. "Do you think I'll see real cows?"

"Something tells me yes. But don't get too close. They're large animals and you could hurt."

Not for the first time today, her son heaved a sigh too heavy for his young years and rolled his eyes at her. "Mom, I want to draw them, not play with them."

"I know. But still."

The kid just shook his head and she wondered for the umpteenth time if there wasn't a thirty-year-old man hidden in her nine-year-old son's body.

A rap sounded on the doorframe. Carson stood smiling at her. Had his eyes always been such a deep blue?

"Mom's baking cookies. She sent me to tell you they'll be ready to eat shortly."

"Cookies?" Colton looked up.

"Chocolate chip and butter cookies."

Tossing his artwork to one side, Colton bounced on the bed. "I love butter cookies."

Surprise registered clearly on Carson's face. "Me too."

On his feet, Colton came to a stop at Carson's side, his gaze settling on his mother, "Coming?"

"Almost done here. You two go on and I'll be down in a second, but save me some chocolate chips."

"Sure thing." Colton grinned and spun about to face Carson. "Last one down stairs is a rotten egg."

Before Carson could say yay or nay, the kid had taken off running down the hall. Her mouth open, she was all set to reprove her son for running in the house when Carson, laughing now, waved her off and took off after their son. Great. Now she was going to have to corral not one but two kids.

In only a few hours, the world simply had to have tilted on its axis. That was the only possible explanation Carson had for why he was sitting in his mother's kitchen with a nine-year-old son and upstairs unpacking was the one woman he's never been truly able to forget. At least for a little while.

"What's your favorite subject?"

Without hesitation, Colton mumbled, "Math" around the bite of another cookie.

His mom, on the other hand, hadn't stopped smiling and was already working on another batch of butter cookies. This kid might go home weighing an extra twenty pounds if the Sweet matriarch kept baking like this.

"Oh, my." Glancing at her watch, Carson's mom stepped away from the bowl of batter and quickly washed her hands. "It's time to check on the calves."

"Calves?" Colton looked up.

"We have two rejected calves in the birthing barn. Garret tried getting one of the moms who lost a calf to adopt them, but it didn't work. Now they have to be bottle-fed. Would you like to come with me?"

"Can I?" Excitement gleamed in the young boy's eyes.

"Of course." His mother tipped her head toward the back door for Colton to follow her. Another moment later the screen door slammed shut behind them and the two were darting toward the barn like a couple of wayward children.

"Where did Colton go?" Jess appeared behind him.

"He and Mom are in the barn with the new calves."

"Is that okay?" Her gaze darted from him to the kitchen door and back. "I mean, I don't want him to bother your mother."

Jillian was the first to laugh. "The way she walked out of here laughing and giggling like a ten year old herself. Doubt it."

"Oh. Well. Maybe I should go check. Just in case."

"Sure." Carson pushed away from the wall. "I'll show you."

To his surprise, when he took a step forward, Jess took a step back. "No. Thank you. Just point me in the direction of the barn and I'm sure even this city girl can find the broad side of it."

Not sure why she didn't want him to accompany her, he simply nodded and pointed. "Follow the path, it'll be pretty obvious."

"Thought so." She smiled and quickly turned to hurry after her son.

The door closed behind her and Rachel spun around. "Okay. Spill. What's going on here?"

"Let's take this into the study." Garrett pushed to his feet. "I'll call Preston."

The sound of stomping boots on the back porch filled the kitchen. All the siblings looked up to see Preston brushing his boots while holding his wife's hand.

"Not bad timing." Garret turned on his heel and walked away.

"Who's the kid on the way to the barn with Mom?" Preston hung his hat on the nearby rack.

"We're heading to the study to find out." Jillian spun around and followed her youngest brother. Her sister on her heels.

Brows dipped with confusion, Preston turned to his wife and back. "Was the question that hard?"

"No," Carson snapped. "But it looks like we're all going to the study."

He'd barely crossed the threshold when Garret settled into his favorite chair and dropped his boot heel over his other knee. "Give."

"Can't a man bring an old friend home for dinner?"

"Of course you can." Jillian poured a cola and handed it to her sister. "Now spill."

"Fine." He wished he'd had more time to process the day's events himself, but here goes nothing. "Jessica and I had a few classes together back at SCHOOL."

"That much you told us." Considering Garret was the youngest of the brothers, right about now he looked like the big brother.

"Let me see if I can make this easier on you." Rachel handed him a beer, then silently asked Preston if he wanted one before handing the other to Garret. "When did you learn that Colton's your son?"

Jillian choked on her cola, Garret's boot slid off his knee and landed on the wooden floor with a heavy thud, and Preston's jaw fell open. "Make mine a bourbon."

"How did you know?" It was the only sensible thing he could say.

Rachel collapsed into the sofa. "You mean besides the fact that he loves the same cookies you do, draws with the same skill you do, and has your smile?"

"Yeah, besides that."

"You look at him as if he were more precious than the crowned jewels."

All heads whipped in his direction.

Why did he feel like a guppy in a fish bowl? Oh yeah—because he just brought home a son he didn't know he had and everyone here wanted answers he didn't have.

CHAPTER FIVE

Alice Sweet wasn't saying a word, but did her son really think she wasn't catching on to what was really going on? Though she had way more questions than answers, she was willing to bet the ranch she loved that this young boy was not just any boy, but a Sweet. What a precious gift after so much loss.

"Would you like to feed him now?"

Colton's eyes widened. "Can I?"

"Sure." Working with him, Alice helped him hold the bottle just right for the young calf to guzzle easily.

His laughter was worth it all.

"Be careful," his mother said.

"It's hard to mess this part up," she reassured Jess. Oh, how she wanted to pepper Jess with questions. What happened? Did my son know? Why am I only meeting my grandson now? Have you been on your own? Was he an easy baby? So many questions.

At least from the way Colton behaved and how Jess eyed her son, any fool could see the child had been well loved.

Oh, Charlie, what did our son do?

"So yes or no?" Preston asked him.

Swallowing hard, Carson nodded. "Yes."

"Why now?" Garret leaned forward. "Why bring him home now?"

"Hey, I've only known about him for a few hours more than you."

"What?" Jillian said a little louder than she'd probably meant to.

"Wait." Garret shook his head and straightened in his seat. "How can you not know you had a son?"

Jillian was the one to shoot her youngest brother a slack-jawed glare. "Really?" she spun around to face Carson. "I'm guessing she didn't tell you?"

He nodded.

"Why wouldn't she tell you?" Garret was frowning now. "What did you do to her?"

"I didn't do anything. It was just one night."

That heavy-booted foot landed on the wood floor again. "Oh, man. I expected more from you."

"We were in college. We had a little too much to drink. We were young." He wasn't going to say he'd been crushing on her since the first day she walked through the door of stats class.

"No excuse," Garret spat, "there are rules, and you broke the most important one."

"Don't hand me that," Carson ground out, "are you going to tell me you spent four years in college and never left your dorm room?"

"Of course not." Garret jumped to his feet and stood toe to toe with Carson. "But no one was drunk, and everyone was protected. Rules."

"I didn't say she was drunk. I said we had a little too much to drink. They are not the same thing."

"The hell, they're not," Garret barked.

"Boys, boys," Preston came between his brothers. "Y'all want to fight this out, do it later, right now, we need to know more of what's going on." He turned to Preston. "Why is she here now?"

"Long story short, her ex-husband has developed Huntington's disease." A few hisses and grimaces could be seen and heard across the room. "When they tested Colton to see if he'd inherited it, Jess learned her ex isn't Colton's father after all. I was the only other option."

"Have you arranged for a DNA test?" Jillian asked.

"Really?" her twin whirled around to face her. "You can't see it."

"Frankly," Jillian shrugged, "no."

Sarah grinned at her sister-in-law. "If it makes you feel any better, I wouldn't have connected the dots either."

"So," Preston grabbed hold of his wife's hand, again. "This will be wedding number two? Mom certainly can't object to you marrying the mother of her grandson, whether you love her or not."

"Did she agree?" Rachel's voice dripped with anticipation.

Jillian's question tripped over her sister's. "That's why she's here then?"

"But," Sarah cut off her in-laws, "I thought you said you only found out a few hours ago. How is she here already?"

Holding up his hands, palms out. "Whoa. One at a time. No, she hasn't agreed because she doesn't know anything about our trust fund dilemma. No, that's not why she's here." He turned to face Sarah. "And she came to tell me in person rather than over the phone or email. We sort of bumped into each other at the café."

"Got it." Sarah nodded. "Now what?"

He dropped his head back against the massive recliner. "I can't just say, thanks for stopping by, oh and as long as you're here, why don't we get married so I can help save the family ranch."

"Why not?" Rachel asked. "People marry because they're having a baby all the time. You'll marry because you already have one. What's so difficult about that?"

"Considering we haven't seen each other in almost ten years, I'd say a lot."

"No worse than marrying a stranger you found off the internet," Jillian pointed out.

"Except when the year is said and done, we'll still share a son."

"He has a point." Rachel shook her head. "How is it everything keeps getting turned on its head around here."

"Tell me about it." Garret. Scrubbed his face. "All right big brother. Now what?"

"You have a nice family." When Jess thought about all the years wasted with Todd and his dysfunctional family, she could almost cry.

"Most of the time, I'll agree with you." Seated in one of the many rockers on the back porch, even after all these years, Jess could tell Carson was hiding behind his smile.

Something told her on any other night, a good portion, if not all, of his siblings would be out here with him, enjoying the light evening breeze. Tonight, she was pretty sure this nice family was giving Carson the space they needed.

"Tell me something." Carson kicked the rocker into motion. "Do you think, if you hadn't gone back to Todd, that we would have had a chance?"

Memories of the last couple of weeks with Carson tugged at the corners of her mouth. "I thought so."

His head bobbed and the chair set to rocking just a tad faster.

"I know they say hindsight is twenty twenty, but even before I learned the truth, I've often wished things could have been different."

Taking a sip of lemonade, Carson nodded and heaved a deep sigh. "Now that you've found me, what are your plans?"

She almost laughed. "Plans aren't my strength. So far every plan I've ever made has fallen flat on its face and impulse has given me the most happiness."

The way his lips tipped upward in a lazy smile, she had the feeling he was thinking of the same things she was; their brief time together ten years ago, and today. "Let me rephrase that." He cleared his throat and forearms resting on his knees, he leaned forward. "Would you consider moving with Colton here to Honeysuckle? We have a growing community, good schools, and lots of family."

Her heart lurched to her throat before settling down to its rightful place. Driving to West Texas had been an impulse, at least that's what she'd told herself. Had this been what she'd really hoped for? A true fresh start? Lord knew, after meeting the rest of the Sweet family, she couldn't picture a better way for her son to grow up.

"I mean, you wouldn't have to sell your house if you didn't want to. We could find a property manager for it."

"I don't own a house."

"Oh." That seemed to surprise him.

"We rent."

"I see. I'd be happy to pay off the remainder of your lease if you'd consider moving here."

She shook her head. "No lease. Month to month." And there was no point mentioning she was short this month's upcoming rent. Or that she'd been downsized out of her job beginning in two weeks.

"I see." His head bobbed and he went back to rocking.

She liked it better when he was asking questions. "If we were to consider relocating."

"Mm," was all he said as the chair swayed back and forth.

"I'd have to find a suitable place to live, a job, and…"

"And?"

"I guess that's the two critical pieces."

Once again, he leaned forward. "I am very willing and usually able to provide for Colton, and you if you need it."

"Usually?"

He heaved another deep sigh. "The ranch has run into a few problems. Dad died a little over a year ago, and suffice it to say, our trusted foreman wasn't so trusted."

"Oh, no." Her hand flattened against her collar bone. "How awful for your mother. I'm so sorry."

"Thank you. The problem is, we've all moved home in an effort to save every penny we can to keep the bank from taking away the ranch."

"I see." Sitting back, her hands clasped in her lap, she found herself rocking back and forth where he had stopped.

"I don't think you do." For the next several minutes, Carson went into great detail about the ranch, the foreman, the thefts, the trust, his brother's fake marriage and the struggles all the siblings were having to do the same. "Of course the hardest part has been pulling the wool over Mom's eyes."

All she could do was nod. This entire scenario sounded like it had fallen from the pages of a really bad made for TV movie script.

"I know it's asking a lot, and I can't quite wrap my head around how to do this without hurting Colton."

"This?"

He stared at her for a while and she could see the exact moment when he realized whatever he was saying and she was hearing may not be the same thing. "I was hoping, perhaps you'd be willing to marry me..."

She was pretty sure her jaw came close to hitting the floor and her eyeballs may have escaped from their sockets. "You want what?"

Frantically, he shook his head. "Not for real. I mean, I wouldn't expect you, I mean, we don't have to, that is..." Pausing, he pinched the bridge of his nose and sighed. "Open mouth insert size thirteen shoe."

Sorting through his rambling, slowly, she began to put the pieces together. He was asking her to do what Sarah had done. To help save the ranch. What she couldn't decide was if this was an answer to prayer, or if she wanted to haul off and belt him.

"Feel free to slug me if it makes you feel better." His gaze softened, but worry still danced in his eyes.

On the other hand, his uncanny ability, even after all these years, to know what she was thinking, made her smile. "I considered it."

Shaking his head, he leaned back again. "It's thoughtless, selfish, and I'm worried about Colton, but I'm also desperate. If you're willing to help, and we put our heads together, I know we can figure out a way to make this work."

CHAPTER SIX

"One of these days I'm going to build a chicken coup and have fresh eggs." Squatting on her haunches, Alice Sweet had a roll of paper towels in one hand and a yellow mess under the other.

"How many?" Carson didn't have to be a gourmet chef to know that this morning's eggs were now splattered on the kitchen floor.

"The whole carton. Eighteen eggs. Slipped right out of my hand, flipped open, and splat." Tossing the gloppy towels into the trash, she pushed to her feet and sighed. "Can you run down to the farmer's market for me? Sadie Thompson is saving two dozen eggs for us."

Carson nodded.

The back door creaked open and Clint, the lone hand, stood in the doorway, hat in hand. "Excuse me ma'am."

Mop in hand, Carson's mom looked up. "If you've come to borrow eggs, you're just plumb out of luck."

"No, ma'am." He shook his head. "I uhm, hate to ask this but I need an afternoon off."

"Of course." She leaned the mop handle against the counter. "Clint, anything you need is yours."

"Thank you, ma'am."

"It's none of my business, but, nothing serious, I hope?"

"No ma'am. Just an appointment that I have to keep."

His mother nodded, but something in the way Clint stood didn't seem like the self-assured man Carson had gotten to know over the last couple of months. The cowhand seemed, almost nervous.

"Morning." Her son in front of her, Jess nudged Colton into the kitchen. "Sorry we're late. I didn't realize how early ranch life starts."

"No, worries. You two sleep in as long as you need to." His mother pulled out a couple of loaves of bread from the drawer.

Hat in hand, Carson nodded at his mother. "I'd better get going."

"Thanks, baby." His mom leaned in for him to kiss her cheek.

"Going?" A hint of panic flickered in Jess's eyes.

"To town. Mom needs more eggs."

Growling deep in her throat, his mother sighed. "Wouldn't need more eggs if I hadn't dropped the carton."

"Oh, no." Jess's gaze darted about the kitchen floor. "Can I help somehow?"

"Actually," his mom straightened and smiled at her. "Why don't you go with Carson, make sure he doesn't get sidetracked."

"Mom." The urge to stomp his feet and remind her he wasn't four years old anymore, was almost overpowering.

"I'd be happy to tag along," Jess cut him off before he said something stupid. "Let me grab my purse." She swung around to face Colton. "You be good."

"I'd best be getting to my chores too." Clint took a step in retreat. "If you'll excuse me."

With Jess at his side, Carson followed the ranch hand out the back door. Something in Clint's gaze made Carson want to take an extra minute to talk to the man. After all, he was doing as much for the ranch as any of the family, with nothing to gain but a good deed. "Hey, Clint."

The man stopped short in his tracks.

"Was just wondering if there's anything I can do to help today?"

Clint's brows buckled at the bridge of his nose. "Help?"

"Well," Carson shrugged. "You've been more than helpful the last few months, and if there's anything I, or my brothers, can do to help, we want you to know, all you have to do is ask."

The man didn't quite smile, but the look in his eyes softened. "Thank you. Appreciate it, but today's just a simple errand."

Carson nodded. "Sounds good, but keep the offer in mind."

"Will do." He turned and headed to a beat up old truck.

Not till now had Carson noticed the man had out of state plates. Not that there was anything unusual about that, but it caught his eye nonetheless.

"Is something wrong?" Jess came to his side.

Shaking his head, he offered a soft smile. "Colton is all right staying behind?"

"Are you kidding? I had no idea my son was a cow lover."

That made Carson chuckle. Regardless of the possibility that ranching ran thick in the Sweet family bloodline, what kid could request a cow-eyed calf? Without thinking, he extended his elbow to her, delighted when she not only slid her hand into the bend of his arm, but smiled up at him. For just a second in time, he was transported back ten years to a couple of free-spirited college kids without a care in the world. For just a moment.

"Where exactly is the grocery store?" Jess hadn't had much time to see the town yesterday, but didn't remember noticing a supermarket while she was there.

"There are a couple of different supermarkets, but we're going to the farmer's market. Mom loves Abigail Fine's fresh eggs, and her honeysuckle wine, but today we're just getting the eggs."

"Honeysuckle wine? I didn't know you can make wine out of honeysuckle."

Carson shrugged. "I think that old expression, where there's a will, there's a way might fit under these circumstances. The town has found a way to make all things honeysuckle. From candles, and wine to syrup and tea. I wouldn't be surprised if someone hasn't thought to make a salad from the plant."

"Salad." Jess was sure her face had to be crinkled like a sharpie puppy at the thought. Of course, she wasn't much of a greens person. Just the mention of arugula could send her hunting for a good donut or steak.

"Did you sleep okay?"

"Very much so." Maybe it was the country air, or the good cooking, or the company, but she couldn't remember sleeping so peacefully and soundly in a very, very long time.

"Good." Quiet settled around them for a few miles when Carson let out a deep sigh. "I think Colton is liking being on the ranch."

"You think?" she smiled. "Not even twenty-four hours and I *know* he loves it."

A wide smile took over his face. "Can't blame him. Can you."

"No." She shook her head and relaxed into the seat. "You always spoke about home with so much love in your voice and eyes. Not just for your family, but the ranch, the land, the history, any fool could see how much you loved your life. Now I've had a little taste of why you love it so much."

"Enough to stay?" The way he casually stared ahead at the road, anyone would think he'd merely mentioned the weather.

Part of her wanted to say, of course I can stay, want to stay, but another part of her wanted to scream, have you lost your mind? I'm a city girl. And just to make herself a little more crazy than she already was, a third part of her whispered in her ear, stay, you shouldn't have to do it all alone. Unfortunately, her tongue felt stuck in a vat of peanut butter.

"I don't mean to sound insensitive, but if I have to get married to save the ranch, the idea of marrying someone I actually like, even if only for appearance's sake, is way more appealing than striking a bargain with a stranger."

Somehow that made a modicum of sense even though none of what was going on with his siblings did. Who married to save a house? Never mind six people all agreeing to do just that. Although, after less than a day on the Sweet Ranch, it made even more sense than it should. What she didn't understand at all, was why wasn't she more upset or offended at an off-handed proposition of marriage? She should be shouting at him, *how dare you*, but she wasn't. Even when she'd told him she'd considered slugging him for suggesting a marriage of convenience, she really hadn't. Maybe all the confusion churning inside of her since learning that Todd was not Colton's father had numbed all her senses, especially, common sense. "You're really going to marry anyone?"

One shoulder lifted in a lazy shrug that reminded her so much of the young man she once thought she could so easily fall in love with. "Not anyone, or I'd be married already."

"Preston and Sarah look very happy."

"They are very happy." Carson blinked slowly, then sighed. "I think that's what makes it harder for the rest of us. We all know that whatever arrangements we make, will be strictly a business deal."

"Is it worth it?"

His head turned to momentarily face her. "The ranch. Probably. My mom. Absolutely. It would kill her to know she's the one who let the family legacy slip away."

"But it's not her fault. Anyone can be taken in by someone they trust."

"I know that. My siblings know that. And maybe you know that. But she'll never believe if she'd asked more questions, stayed more hands on, something, anything, then Ray wouldn't have been able to rob us all blind."

In a very odd way, she understood how Alice Sweet felt. What if instead of assuming Todd was the father, she'd said something to Carson? What if she'd not married the wrong man simply because she was pregnant and scared and just raised her son on her own? What if she'd given Carson and herself a little more time to see where things could have gone? "Do you ever think about us?"

Silence never sounded so loud. What possessed her to ask such a thing?

Slowly, his head bobbed. "Not as much in recent years. But when you left, I missed you—a lot. Your laugh. The way you always poked me when I'd frown at the professor. It was hard losing my friend."

"We were good friends." The memories made her smile. Until she'd started poking him, he didn't even realize that he would frown at the professors when he either didn't like what they said, or didn't agree, or had simply been distracted and struggled to catch up. Gently, she'd jab him with a pencil or her finger, depending on where he was sitting. "I missed you too."

Once again, he turned to face her, his gaze darted from the road ahead, back to her. "Tell me the truth. If you and Colton pack up and return to where you came from, will you be all right?"

Wasn't that a loaded question.

"That's what I thought." He sighed again and stared quietly at the road ahead. "Look. I want to be a father in Colton's life, but it's going to be hard as hell if I'm in Honeysuckle and you're in Oklahoma. You don't have to take me up on my crazy offer for a temporary marriage, but at least consider moving here. We can find you work and place to live, and we'll find a way to make it all work."

How long had it been since she'd had a partner and not a problem.

Carson pulled into a parking space by the outdoor market cluttered with colorful umbrellas, small tables and booths, and all sorts of fresh foods and, was that homemade mozzarella hanging from a stand?

It was clear to any idiot that Colton liked the ranch, he'd already learned that the kids in town were friendly, and so far, Alice Sweet was the perfect grandmother. How awful could it be to move to small-town USA? "Carson?"

His hand on the door handle, he paused with the door ajar. "Yes."

"What would happen after the year?"

CHAPTER SEVEN

Was Jess asking what Carson thought she was? Could it be that she was actually considering marrying him for the trust? Either way, in the middle of town was no place to have this conversation. Pulling the door closed, he turned to her, trying desperately to form the correct words before opening his mouth. "Are we talking about what I think we're talking about?"

"That depends on what you think I think we're thinking about."

Whatever tension had been building inside him completely washed away and in a matter or only a few words, he was chuckling to himself, transported back to college, back to an easier time, and back to just him and the only woman he's never been able to forget. "Jessica NAME, you are amazing."

"I know." Her smile widened as the sparkle in her eyes brightened. "Seriously, if we were to marry to save the ranch, what happens after the first anniversary and the big payout? I realize we get a divorce, but by then, Colton will be used to living on the ranch and being part of the Sweet family."

How to sober a man quickly. He knew this was the bigger problem, but he hadn't quite thought it through, not to mention, he had zero parenting skills, at least for now. "Other than, Colton is a part of the Sweet family and will always be a part of the family, I haven't quite gotten that far."

"Colton is my number one priority. I would like to help you, and your family, to save the ranch, but not if Colton is the one to pay the price."

He hadn't been a father very long, but already he agreed with her. For the same reason his mother would never let her kids marry for money if she knew what they were all up to, he could never do anything to hurt his son. Dang, those words still sent shockwaves in his brain every time he thought them. *His son.* Sucking in a deep breath and blowing it out ever so slowly, he reached for the handle again. "Let's get the eggs, and let me think this through a little better."

"You mean us, right?"

The softness of her smile coaxed a lazy grin from him in response. "I mean us. We'll think it through." Especially since marriage for money or not, they had a lot to work out about their son.

"Look." Vicki jabbed her sister Liz in the ribs. "Carson is coming this way and there's a woman with him."

Shorter than her, Liz inched up on her tippy toes to see. "You think that's *her*?"

Resisting the urge to roll her eyes at her younger sibling, Vicki settled for a soft sigh. "Who else do you think would be arriving in town with Carson at this hour of the day?"

"Good point." Liz nodded.

"Quick." Grabbing hold of the corner of her sister's t-shirt, Vicki tugged Liz to her side. "They're coming this way."

"Ooh," Liz squealed gleefully.

All her sister needed to be over the top happy was a blinged out corn hole accessory, or a female stranger in town with one of her nephews. Of course in this case, Liz had good reason to be excited as well as curious. Alice had called them late last night and told them about the new unexpected houseguest and her son. A son that Alice was willing to bet the whole shebang was Carson's.

"Hi there." Vicki waved at her nephew. "Don't usually

see you here."

"Mom needs eggs. I ran into town quick to pick some up for her." Noticing both his aunts watching Jess, he took a step back. "Aunt Vicki, Liz, this is an old school friend, Jess."

"How do you do?" Smiling, Jess shook each woman's hand.

"Nice to have you here, dear," Liz beamed at Jess until her sister jabbed her in the ribs.

"You'd better run along and get the eggs. Wouldn't want your mother blaming us for your showing up late."

Carson leaned in, kissed Vicki on the cheek, waved at Liz behind her booth, and walked away with Jess at his side.

"I like her." Liz nodded her head.

"All she said was nice to meet you. How can you like her with only four words exchanged?"

Liz shrugged at her older sister. "I just do."

Staring after her nephew already at the egg booth, Vicki sighed. She sure hoped Carson liked the pretty woman too.

"They're cute." Who knew shopping for eggs could be so entertaining.

Carson took the change for the eggs and squinted at her. "The eggs?"

Chuckling, Jess shook her head. "Your aunts. They've been watching us the whole time and the taller blonde... Vicki?"

He nodded.

"Vicki keeps poking Liz in the ribs, probably reminding her not to stare."

"Aunt Vicki is the oldest of the three sisters, sometimes she can be, well, a little bossy." Taking two steps forward, Carson paused and looked down at her, his gaze darting over her shoulders to his aunts down the way. "What do you say we give them something to talk about?"

Her eyes popped open before the teasing glint in his

eyes made her smile. "What do you have in mind?"

Without saying a word, he reached for her hand, threaded their fingers together, and smiled. "Is this okay?"

"It's not nice to tease your aunts." She softened her words with a tilt of her head and flash of a smile.

"Sorry." Pulling his hand away, he shoved it quickly in his pocket. "I guess for a moment I forgot I wasn't back in high school."

A few things rushed through her mind. The first, how she desperately wished she'd said anything else so he would still be holding her hand. The other, an unexpected longing to have lived in this small town and seen what Carson Sweet was like back in high school, over took all common sense. The small part of her brain shouting at her to use common sense, be practical, behave like an adult, got shoved aside by the longing to hold his hand again. Before she could talk herself out of it, she'd snatched his wrist from his pocket and laced her fingers with his. "Maybe a little teasing won't hurt."

The smile that bloomed across his face made her stomach flutter as if invaded by a flock of trapped butterflies. Next thing she knew, they'd practically skipped to the truck and she had no choice but to let go if she was going to climb in and let him drive them back to the ranch.

"I'm sorry." He looked at her as he snapped his seat belt in place.

"For what?"

"For not thinking."

"Excuse me?" She wasn't following his train of thought at all. That realization made her a little sad. Once upon a time she almost always knew what he was thinking. Funny how she never gave that little thing between them any thought. She never knew what Todd was thinking. Not when they were dating, not when they were married, and even less since the divorce. She should have realized just how special what they had was. Too bad that was so long ago. "I'm not following?"

"Well," he chuckled softly before sighing. "Not only did my aunt see us, but so did half the gossips in town. I wasn't thinking."

"You really have town gossips?"

He blinked at her a moment before returning his gaze to the street and pulling out of the parking space. "We most definitely have gossips. Most likely, I suspect they were town criers in a previous lifetime. Not only will they tell all their friends and neighbors that they saw me holding hands with a woman, they'll tell their enemies too. There won't be a soul in Honeysuckle who hasn't heard about us by tomorrow morning."

"I see." Which brought them full circle to what the heck were they going to do about the ranch, his dilemma, and the son they shared?

Why did life have to be so hard? As a kid he could hardly wait to grow up and be an adult. To get his license, finish high school, be legal to vote, to drink, and to play with the big boys in the real estate world. Now, not for the first time, he acknowledged that adulting isn't all it's cracked up to be.

"Let's set the Sweet family problems aside."

"Okay," she nodded.

"First thing I need to understand. Todd has raised Colton for nine years. They must have a bond of some kind."

Jess merely rolled her eyes. "Todd never bonded with Colton. He didn't like babies, wasn't much happier about a toddler, and remained indifferent as Colton grew."

"You did mention something about that, but I thought, I don't know." If he'd found so much delightful about a little boy, he'd known less than twenty-four hours, he had a hard time believing that any man could spend nine years with the boy and not feel something. "He is Colton's legal father. You were married when he was born. That has to come into play."

She shook her head again. "He's already signed away all his parental rights. Basically, he and his mother both told me they wanted nothing to do with another man's…er," she cleared her throat. "Son."

From the way spitting those words out had her squirming in her seat, something told him that the jerk hadn't been quite so polite about stepping aside. "So, how does Colton feel? Even the guy would never win a father-of-the-year award, Colton must miss him."

"I don't think so."

"You don't think?"

One shoulder hefted up in a lazy shrug. "Deep down he might, but I'm not seeing any signs. Colton doesn't ask where his father is, doesn't ask what he's doing, doesn't ask to see Todd. Before I knew the truth, I told him his daddy was very sick, wasn't himself anymore, and would be going to live in heaven soon."

"How'd he take it then?"

"Fine. Just said maybe Todd would be happier in heaven."

"How old is this kid?" Carson couldn't resist the snarky retort. "Sorry. He seems wiser than his years."

"Always has been. I remember when he was about three years old, Todd had had a little too much to drink and was grumbling and ranting about leaving a door open and the cost of electricity and he didn't own a power house, etc., etc. Colton looked up at me from the kitchen table where he was coloring and softly told me; *Daddy's having a hard day.* As if that would help me understand."

So much impressed him about Colton, despite his tender years, but now, now Carson was blown away. "He's an amazing boy."

That brought a wide grin to Jess's face. "I think so."

"All right. Then what we need to work out is what lies ahead. I've asked it before, but I'll ask again. Do you think you could be happy living in a small town? Because that's the easiest way for me to be a part of Colton's everyday life."

"I don't honestly know. I'm a city girl. If I run out of milk, or eggs, I can get any number of grocery stores in less than five minutes. If I'm in the mood to shop for something to cheer me up, there are three major malls within a few minutes' drive. Same for movies, take your pick which theater you want to go to. I've never lived in a town where gossip can spread like wild fire."

He knew exactly what she was talking about. The hustle and bustle of the bigger cities had both drawn him in, giving him a reason to leave home, and in time, given him a reason to move back to the simpler way of life.

"Is I'm willing to try good enough of an answer?"

His head bobbed. Willing to try was something he could work with. "I haven't asked. What do you do for a living?"

"I'm a teacher's aide. Never did finish my degree."

Again, he nodded. That he could work with. Even small towns had schools.

"Then let's start there. One step at a time."

Her mouth tipped into another sweet smile. "One step at a time."

Now all he had to do was keep himself from rushing. Maybe, if he took his time, everything would fall into place. He could only hope.

CHAPTER EIGHT

"Wow. Dinosaur pancakes!" Colton's eyes lit up like a kid on Christmas morning. "Mom just makes ordinary round."

"It's been a long time since I made animal-shaped pancakes." Spatula in hand, Carson's mom smiled at the boy before flipping another pancake. "It's nice to try again."

"Hey, slow down." Jess's gently patted her son's arm. "This isn't a race."

"Your mother is right," the family matriarch's grin slipped slightly in an effort to look a bit more serious. "It's important for your health to chew your food well. Besides, there's plenty more where those came from." Her motherly, or in this case grandmotherly, speech over, a wide grin was back on her face.

"Yes, ma'am. Sorry."

The way Carson's mother's smile bloomed and her eyes sparkled, anyone would think the kid had just told his grandmother that there was gold buried in the backyard.

"While y'all were getting us more fresh eggs," Alice Sweet waved the spatula at her son, "Colton and I took a detour into the attic. We brought down your old telescope."

"You still have that?" Why it surprised him that his mother would have stashed every tidbit of their childhood in the attic, he didn't know.

"Yes," her voice dropped an octave in modulated reproof. "There was an alignment of planets last night and if we hurry, I bet it can still be seen, with the telescope, from the canyon bed."

"That's a great idea." Her empty dish in hand, Rachel stepped away from the table.

"Of course it is." His mother smiled at Colton.

"Canyon?" Jess asked softly.

"It's not really much of a canyon," Jillian slipped her plate into the dishwasher.

"We've got a lot of work scheduled for today," Colton hated to be the one to smother a fun idea, but he carried the majority of the load since all his other siblings had day jobs to run off after early ranch chores. "Maybe we could do it another time."

The way his mother shook her head, Carson knew there was more to be said.

His mom's pointed glare was directed solely at him. "Another time would be in about twenty years."

Garrett pushed away from the table. "I've got all day. I'm sure Clint and I can do without you for a few hours."

"If we're riding out to the canyon, that'll be more than a few hours." Whether he was shirking his responsibilities to the ranch or to Colton, either way, Carson had a huge slice of guilt on his plate.

"Riding?" Once again Jess's eyes rounded, at the moment a little wider than the time before.

"If you take the jeep, it will save some time." Garret slid his dishes into the sink. "It still might make for a long day, but it will be easier on everyone."

By everyone, Carson knew his brother meant Jess and their son. Especially since he was pretty sure neither of them had likely been on a horse. Ever. At least not a real one.

"I don't know." And Carson really had no idea what was the responsible thing to do—he couldn't shake the idea that either way, he'd be letting someone down.

"Your brother is right," his mother's gaze bore through him. "You take Colton and Jess out in the jeep, set up the telescope, and enjoy the view, and the day. I've already got a nice lunch packed for you."

Of course she did. His mother had always believed in an ounce of prevention is worth a pound of cure, or in this case, an ounce of preparation is a guarantee to get her way. Still uncomfortable passing off his chores, Carson scanned the room, every sibling here gave a brief and sure nod of their heads. "I guess we're going star gazing."

"Planet gazing," his mother corrected, roughly WORD the top of Colton's head.

He had to be a good boy to simply look up at the woman he had no idea was his grandmother and smile at her for mussing his hair. Could it be having been raised by Todd had left the poor kid craving any attention?

Slowly, Carson's fingers curled at his sides. While he'd been less than happy to realize that he had missed out on so much in his son's life, the harsh reality that Colton's childhood had been lacking thanks to Todd's indifference left Carson ready to shove a fist through the nearest wall, not that it would change anything for the better, but the anger was still there.

"Carson?" Jess's hand rested gently on his forearm. "Is something wrong?"

"Wrong?"

Her voice dropped as she leaned slightly closer. "That vein in your forehead is popping. It always did that when you were upset."

Had she really known him that well? Was there anyone else on the planet, including his own family, who could read him so easily? If Jess were to go along with the crazy one-year plan for the sake of the ranch, and some security for her and Colton, would he be able to pull it off? Was there any chance in hell that he could watch her walk away from his life once again? Could he actually let her go?

If anyone had told Jess just a few weeks ago that she and her son would be on the Sweet Ranch in West Texas, riding a jeep to some canyon to watch planets line up for a once every few decades event, she would have asked the person what had they been smoking. And yet, here she was, bouncing across the prairie and despite her big city upbringing, actually looking forward to the adventure.

From the look on her son's face, he was more excited than all of them put together, including Alice Sweet.

"Sit back sweetie." Even though Colton was strapped in with the seat belt, he'd still been leaning so far forward in the passenger seat that Jess had visions of Carson coming to a fast stop and her son flying through the windshield, or at least, snapping forward like a bungee cord.

"Yes, ma'am." Colton turned to Carson. "How much further?"

"Not very."

"This is a really big ranch, isn't it?" Her son's gaze scanned the horizon from left to right.

"One of the biggest in the area."

"I don't see very many cows. Didn't someone say this was a cattle ranch?"

Even from the back seat, Jess could see Carson's face tense. That thin muscle twitching in his jaw.

"It still is. We had a few… incidents over that last year or so, but soon we'll be running more cattle again."

Colton's head bobbed up and down, the smile never leaving his face. The boy had no idea the nightmare that had befallen the Sweet family, and only now, looking at the expanse of land before him and the lack of cattle anywhere within sight, brought home to her just what was at stake for this lovely family.

"This should do it." Carson brought the vehicle to a slow stop. "It won't take long to set up."

"I'll get the picnic basket." Jess hopped out of the back seat and hurried around to where Carson now stood pulling out the telescope and some miscellaneous attachments. It didn't take much experience to see that Colton was all set to rush off and explore the wide open spaces. "Sweetie, why don't you carry the blanket for Mommy?"

Stopping in his tracks, Colton did a one eighty and hurried to where his mom stood. "Sure, Mommy."

Another few minutes and Colton was practically dancing in place. His father at his side, showing him how to adjust and focus the telescope. *His father.* Anyone would think she'd need more time to get used to calling Carson her son's father, and yet, it seemed to roll easily off her tongue. She would forever be asking herself how had she not figured this parental thing out on her own a long time ago.

The more she thought about it, and the more she watched her son interact not only with Carson but all the Sweets, the more she realized that Colton and Carson needed time. Not just a few minutes here and there, not just every other weekend, or every Wednesday night like divorced parents. The two had years of catching up to do. Lost time to make up for. She still wasn't sure a fake marriage was the answer, but at the moment, she didn't have any better ideas either.

"Mommy, look!" His eye glued to the telescope, Colton didn't bother to move his head, he merely waved in the direction his mother sat and urged her to come close to him.

Stepping into the spot that Colton had occupied a moment ago, Jess closed one eye and tried to focus. "Oh, my."

"Isn't it cool?" Colton grinned from ear to proverbial ear.

Her son was right. Seeing five planets lined up in single file was seriously cool. The sort of thing she'd only expect to see on a calendar.

"The last two aren't fully lined up," Carson added, "but they probably will be within a few hours."

Colton looked up at Carson and flashed a delighted toothy grin. "Can we stay to see it?"

With an equally bright smile and a slight bob of his head, Carson concurred with his son. "Absolutely, that's what we're here for."

Another few moments of following the stars, or planets, and Colton seemed to grow a little restless. Staring off in the distance, he pointed ahead. "What's over there?"

"That's the canyon."

"Like the Grand Canyon?"

That made Carson chuckle. "Not exactly. Though the canyon was formed by what was once a river—"

"It's not a river anymore?" Colton interrupted.

"Just a creek. That canyon was probably formed a

bazillion years ago, long before settlers started ranching."

"Can I go look?"

The way Carson's brows buckled made Jess wonder if there was something more dangerous out there than just falling over the edge.

"We can all walk over. Just give me a second."

While Colton went back to studying the sky through the telescope, Jess kept her gaze on Carson as he walked to the Jeep, leaned into the front seat and then straightening to his full height, tucked his shirt in behind him. Except, it wasn't just his shirt he was straightening. It took her another moment or two to add two and two together and realize he'd grabbed a gun and was tucking more than his shirt into his jeans at his back. The hair on the back of her neck rose to stand on end, and she considered maybe life alone, just the two of them, in the city, wasn't such a bad thing.

"Ready?" Carson asked, his gaze settling on Colton.

Jumping back from the telescope, and bolting upright, Colton danced in place. "Ready."

"Okay." Carson waved his son over. "Stay near me and your mom. Now that we're not grazing large herds of cattle, the grass is a little high—"

"Snakes?" Rather than the expected fear on her son's face, Colton cut off Carson, his voice energized by boyhood curiosity, and if Jess wasn't mistaken, hopeful to run into the slithering creatures.

A wide smile bloomed on Carson's face. Jess might even call it pride. "That's right. So we'll all walk together and watch our steps."

Unlike her son, Jess had not one iota of interest in stumbling across a snake. If she could, she'd crawl into Carson's arms and get her feet way off the ground. Or better yet, climb back into the Jeep and not stop driving till she struck Dallas.

Relieved not to have had any incident with snakes or any other unwelcome visitor, Jess looked up and down the length of small canyon. Carson had been right. When she thought of canyons, she envisioned images of the Grand Canyon or the TEXASPARK canyons. This one was definitely deep enough to qualify as a canyon, and she certainly wouldn't want to fall off the edge to the drop below, but she could see someone climbing out of the deep furrow if they did happen to have the misfortune of falling down.

"Oh, wow." Colton trotted away, quickly approaching the edge.

"Take it easy," Carson called out before she could say anything. "Not too close. The ground along the edge may not be very stable."

Just what Jess didn't want to hear. Now images flashed in her mind, over and over, of Colton tumbling down the canyon.

"Relax," Carson lowered his voice and leaned into her. "He's a smart kid, he'll be careful."

One side of her wanted to snap at him that there were probably plenty of smart people who had fallen off cliffs, while another side of her wondered how could he be so confident. There wasn't an ounce of worry in his eyes.

"You didn't say you had horses." Colton pointed down the canyon with one arm while simultaneously twisting to grin at Carson.

"Horses?" The crease that formed between his brows surprised Jess.

"They're beautiful. Can I draw them?" Colton glanced down at his feet. Clearly eager to move closer for a better view of the horses, but not wanting to disobey Carson's instructions.

Carson came to a stop beside his son. "Well, I'll be."

"What?" Jess and Colton echoed in perfect unison.

"Those are wild horses. I didn't think any herds had crossed into Texas."

"Wild?" Jess knew here eyes were probably threatening to fall out of their sockets.

"Mustangs?" Colton's enthusiasm seemed to be spiking.

"Unlikely, but you never know."

"Can we go down and get a closer look?"

Carson shook his head. "It's never a good idea to get too close to any wild animal, whether it's a horse, a buffalo, or a feral cat or dog. Animal instinct for self-preservation can be a problem."

"Don't touch the fluffy cows," Colton deadpanned.

A loud roar of laughter burst out as Carson kicked his head back. "Something like that."

"I'm sorry," Jess interrupted. "Fluffy cows?"

Carson nodded. "You see that everywhere up near Yellowstone and other places with large herds of bison or buffalo."

Jess turned to her son. "Where did you learn that?"

"At school. Mary Margaret O'Hanlon wore a t-shirt with that slogan on it after her family went on a Spring break vacation to Mount Rushmore."

"Is the canyon your land?" Jess asked.

Carson shook his head. "Our property ends at the cliff's edge, the actual canyon and water belongs to the state of Texas, the other side is the Callahan spread."

"So the horses belong to the state?" Jess asked.

"At the moment," Carson squinted in the direction of the herd mulling about, "I'm not sure who they belong to."

"They're beautiful." His gaze glued to the horses below, Colton hadn't moved an inch. "Sure wish I could sketch them."

"We have work horses on the ranch, you're welcome to sketch those if you like." Carson's gaze was focused on the equines, just like his son.

As a matter of fact, from where Jess stood, the resemblance between the two was suddenly quite startling. Their stance, their focus, their profile. Good Lord, how could she not find a way to keep these two together?

CHAPTER NINE

Hanging out all afternoon and evening with Colton and Jess had been the best day Carson Sweet had spent in a hell of a long time. Exhausted, Colton had fallen asleep in the Jeep just before they'd reached home. The kid slept like a proverbial log. Carson lifted him out of the vehicle, carried him into the house and up the stairs to his room and he didn't move a muscle. His mother stripped him of his shoes and pants and Colton didn't even blink. Carson would kill to sleep that soundly.

The plan for the morning was to introduce his son to the horses. Even though a few of the horses would be out working with his siblings and Clint, there would be enough horses left for Colton to meet and sketch.

At the sink, his mom hummed softly as she poured hot water into a pitcher of tea bags. Thinking back, he was pretty sure this was the first time he'd heard his mother humming since they'd found his father slumped at the kitchen table over a year ago. Standing at her side, scrolling through her phone, his sister Rachel frowned.

"Bad news?" he asked.

Rachel shook her head. "Just work."

With a nod his head turned to see the woman sitting at the table, her COLOR hair clipped into a bun with loose strands caressing her shoulders, a little messy but somehow perfect. Cradling a mug of hot coffee, her gaze remained on their son, sitting across from her, scribbling furiously in sketch pad. Their son. Would he ever tire of those words?

Carson tried not to stare, but it was impossible not to feel the tug in his chest every time he looked at the boy. Nine years old, wiry, with his mom's brilliant green eyes and determined jaw line. Shaking away the growing nostalgia, he inched closer to Colton.

"May I see?"

Nodding, Colton sat back so Carson could see. It took a moment but he realized Colton had not just sketched a horse in a pen, but their pen.

"Do you like it?" The little boy's voice sounded smaller than usual.

"Very much."

"It's here. There was a horse outside when I woke up."

"I can tell. It's Cinnamon." The drawing was so good from a distance, he couldn't imagine what the boy could do up close and personal. "This is great."

Colton beamed.

"So." Carson pushed to his feet. "You ready to meet the horses?"

"Am I." Clutching the pad to his chest, the kid sprang to his feet with unexpected speed and flexibility.

"We could see them later if you want to keep drawing." Jess's voice cracked ever so slightly.

It suddenly occurred to him that Jess was a city girl. For all he knew, this was her first time in ranch country. Facing her, he took a step closer. "Have you ever ridden a horse?"

Jess shook her head.

Okay. "But you've seen one before?"

"Does television count?"

"You never went to a dude ranch or a rodeo?"

Nibbling slightly on her lower lip, she shook her head.

All right. Maybe it was Jess he needed to worry about and not Colton. "Then you're in for a treat."

Heaving in a sigh, she nodded, and mumbled, "Treat. Right."

Coming in closer, he leaned into her and lowered his voice. "It will be fine. I promise."

And with that, the three of them stepped out into the sunlight, heading toward the barn. Jess's apprehension was palpable. Her hands rubbed down the side of her jeans and back again.

Effervescing eagerness, Colton scurried several feet

ahead of them.

"Remember the rules." Concern heightened in Jess eyes. "I can't help you if I can't reach you. Wait for us."

Leaning against her, he lowered his voice. "There really isn't much trouble he can get into out here."

"It's not out here I'm worried about." Her gaze remained on Colton and his slower pace.

"Have I ever lied to you?"

That seemed to bring her short. Slowing her steps, she tipped her head to level her gaze with his. He could almost see the wheels turning the pages of time. "No. No, I don't think you ever have."

"Then trust me. He'll be fine."

The scent hit Jess first: earthy, a little dusty, and distinctly animal. She hesitated at the entrance to the stable, her hand resting on the weathered wooden beam. Peering inside, her heart did a nervous flutter at the sound of shuffling hooves and an occasional low, throaty snort. Her gaze darting left then right, she spotted Colton, jaw hanging slightly open, slowly walking, taking in his surroundings. All set to remind Colton to stay close, something she'd taught him as a toddler, terrified he might dart out in front of a moving car on the street or in a parking lot, or succumb to some human predator, she made sure he understood that if she couldn't reach him to help him, then he was too far away. The words were at the tip of her tongue when Carson's words echoed in her head; *trust me.*

She turned to see Carson at her side; his gaze fixed on Colton, his cowboy hat tipped just enough to shadow his pleased smile. "Stop there," he called out. "That first horse is Boots. She's a real sweetie."

As told, Colton came to a stop, the horse nodding her head as if greeting the small human.

"You ready to see your first horse up close and personal?" Carson smiled at her looking entirely too at ease for a man who'd just promised to introduce her to creatures the size of small trucks.

"Define 'ready,'" she resisted the urge to take a step in retreat.

Carson chuckled. His boot heels clicking against the floor with every step. "You've got this, city girl. Just stick close to me."

"That's the plan," she muttered under her breath as he gestured for her to follow.

Dimly lit, the closer they drew to the stalls, the cooler the building felt. Slivers of sunlight cut through the gaps in the wooden planks. And there was her first horse. Boots was gigantic. Noting other horses popping their heads out over the stall doorways, she realized Boots wasn't the only enormous equine—they were all frighteningly large. Mid step, she froze, her jaw struggling to move. "Oh my gosh, they're huge."

"You should see the Clydesdales. Now, *those* are huge animals."

"Thanks, but no thanks." She gestured helplessly at the nearest horse, a massive chestnut creature with a mane that shimmered under the dim stable lights. Boots turned her head to look at Jess. Dark eyes seemed unnervingly intelligent. She wasn't sure who was sizing up who, but right now it seemed the horse was doing all the thinking.

"Good morning Boots." Carson gave the horse a friendly pat on the neck. "She's one of the gentlest ones we've got. Come closer and say hello."

Colton didn't hesitate, walking straight up to where Carson had gestured. She, on the other hand, didn't move. "I'm not sure Boots got the memo about 'gentle.' She looks like she could snap me like a toothpick if she wanted."

Carson laughed outright, the deep, rich sound echoing through the stable. "Trust me, Boots is probably more scared of you than you are of her."

Shaking her head, Jess was pretty sure that's what everyone said about a rattlesnake before it struck.

Extending his hand, Carson motioned for her to come closer. "C'mon. Just take it slow. Horses can sense if you're nervous."

"Great," she mumbled. "What you're saying is that I'm more or less just a walking anxiety beacon."

"She wouldn't hurt a fly, Mom." Colton failed to show even a modicum of concern.

"Remember what I told you before leaving the house." The statement was directed at Colton.

"Yes. Stay away from the hind legs, and don't approach straight in front because their eyes are to the side of their head and I could spook her."

"That's right. Now remember the carrots."

Pulling a large carrot chunk from his pocket, Colton opened his palm, leaving his hand flat and letting Boots nibble it out of his hand. The toothy grin that took over his face as the carrot disappeared had Jess grinning as well.

"She's so soft." Colton rubbed his hand gently down the side of the animal's neck.

Tess dared to take a step closer, her shoes barely making a sound. She could do this. Maybe if she told herself that often enough, she'd actually believe it.

"Come on, Mom. She's a sweetie."

Carson put his hand to his mouth, doing a poor job of hiding his laughter at Colton's repeating what had been said earlier about Boots.

She'd managed to muster the courage to take another step when Boots decided this would be a great time wiggle his lips, bob his head down then up, and let out a snort that had Jess jumping back the two feet she'd suffered to gain.

"You're doing fine," Carson encouraged.

What she couldn't decide was who was eyeing who more closely, her or the horse.

The horse sniffed in her direction, lowering its massive head slightly.

Why couldn't Carson have been an accountant or engineer in some reasonably big city. It didn't have to be bustling like New York or Chicago, but just a little less… horsy.

"Do what I did, Mom. Hold your hand out and give her a carrot. She likes that."

Right, hold out her ordinary hand in front of a large-toothed, lip-smacking behemoth.

"Like this." Carson opened his hand the same way Colton had moments ago, then taking her hand in his, pulled gently at her fingers until her hand was flat, palm up. Then he placed the large carrot piece on her hand. Not letting go, he eased her hand under the horse's nose.

A slight tremble moved her hand. Boot's warm breath puffed against her fingers. Letting out a sharp yelp, she jerked her hand back and away.

Taking hold of her hand, Carson gave it a gentle squeeze. "He's just saying hello. Try again. You're doing fine."

This time, Jenna steeled herself, extended her hand again, and tried not to flinch as the horse's velvety nose brushed against her palm.

"Oh wow," she practically whispered. "She is soft."

"Told ya, Mom." Colton continued rubbing at Boot's neck. The two were becoming fast friends.

"Yeah, Mom," Carson whispered at her ear, his soft breath sending a whole different kind of chill down her spine. "We told you."

Her heart slamming a rapid beat against her rib cage, she let out a soft sigh. If she could stay calm long enough to pat the neck of an animal large enough to swallow her whole, without having a heart attack, maybe she'd figure out how to stand this close to Carson without melting into a pool of quivering nerves. Then again, maybe some day pigs would fly.

CHAPTER TEN

"I'd swear that horse knows he's being sketched." Jess sat on a bay of hale, watching her son hard at work.

"Don't kid yourself." Carson held back a chuckle. "Boots totally knows she's the center of Colton's attention. And she's loving it."

Jess's shoulders shook with amusement. "I don't think I'm going to argue with you. I just can't believe the horse hasn't moved a muscle since Colton started sketching. I don't even think she's twitched an ear."

He knew that Boots would be the right horse to appeal to Colton and put Jess at ease. Most of the night he'd been kicking around the changes that were happening faster than he could process. Even though having Jess and Colton here was new and different and even strange in many ways, everything felt completely right. "I've been thinking."

"Yes." Jess's gaze remained on her son.

"I need to tell my mother." He cleared his throat. "About Colton."

Jess dipped her chin in a short nod.

"Everything else aside, no matter what happens next, Colton is her grandson and she deserves to know sooner than later."

"I know you're right." Her gaze darted momentarily from Colton to Carson and then back again. "And I know that she's nothing like Todd's mother…"

"But you don't want another grandmother to reject him?"

A hint of a smile pulled at one corner of her mouth. "You always did seem to know what I was thinking before I said anything."

No matter how many women he'd met or dated, he'd never found the same connection as he'd once shared with Jess.

"Oh. Mornin'." Clint led his horse into the stable. "Didn't expect to find anyone here at this hour."

Carson lifted his chin in Colton's direction. "Artist at work."

For the first time since he'd met Clint, the ranch hand actually smiled. "Your mother showed me a picture the boy drew for her yesterday. He's good."

Was it normal for a man to feel his heart fill his chest when someone complimented his son? "Very good." Dragging his thoughts to Clint and the horse, he walked into the barn instead of riding, Carson narrowed his gaze. "What brings you back this early?"

"I think he's got a stone in his shoe."

Colton's head popped up. "In his shoe?" the kid's gaze settled on the horse's hooves.

"You want to help me clean out his hoof?" Clint waved his thumb over his shoulder at the horse.

"Can I?" Wide-eyed, Colton looked to his mother and to Carson's delight, his gaze darted momentarily to Carson.

That unsettled look from earlier was back on Jess's face. Nibbling on her lower lip, she glanced at Carson. Understanding her silent question, he nodded at her. Shifting her attention to the ranch hand, she straightened her shoulders. "If you're sure he won't be in your way?"

"No, ma'am. I'd be happy to show him how to put a horse away."

Again, her head snapped around to face Carson, and again he nodded, doing his best to offer a reassuring smile. "Okay, then," she sighed. "I guess Colton is going to learn about horses today."

"Come on," he patted the small of her back, "let's go find my mother."

"Right. Your mother."

He wished she looked more sure than he felt. There was no doubt in his mind that his mother would be thrilled at a grandchild, but he was also pretty sure she wasn't going to be overjoyed that Carson had been an absentee father for so many years. Not that it was his fault. It wasn't really anyone's fault. Just a little joke the universe played on them.

"Are we going to tell the whole family?" Jess kept pace beside him.

"No. My siblings already know. Well, not Kade, but everyone else."

Her head bobbed. "I see."

"I'm not sure why I waited to tell Mom."

Tipping her head to one side, and closing one eye, she stared at him. "You really don't know?"

Did he?

"You wanted more time to absorb it yourself."

And she did it again. "Maybe. Yeah, I needed to feel more at home with everything before I broke the news to Mom. And maybe, just a little fear."

Jess stopped short. "Fear? *That* I don't understand."

"Garret railed into me pretty harshly about how everything came to be. I suppose I didn't want to see the same reaction in Mom's eyes."

She kept walking. "No matter how old we get, we always want our parents' approval."

Stepping onto the back porch, Carson sucked in a deep breath and glanced at the mother of his son. "Ready?"

"Not sure I'll ever be ready, but this is as good as you're going to get."

Holding the door open, he couldn't help but chuckle. "I'll take it." With a wave of his arm, she entered the kitchen first and he resisted the urge to grab hold of her hand. "Hi Mom."

As soon as Jess and Carson crossed the threshold into the kitchen, his mother looked up at them and then over their shoulder. "Where's Colton?"

"Clint is showing him how to groom and put away a horse."

His mother's smile blossomed more than Jess would have expected from such a simple comment.

"Isn't that wonderful," Alice Sweet slapped her hands together. "He's going to be a rancher."

Carson's eyes circled wide. "That may be a stretch."

With a casual shrug, Carson's mom grinned and reached for a tea kettle. "I was just making a cup, would you two like one."

"That would be lovely, but I can do it." Jess stepped forward, but Alice waved her back.

"It's not that hard to pour."

"Actually," Carson pulled another mug from the cupboard, "I wanted to talk to you about something." Setting the mug on the counter, he took the kettle from his mother. "I mean, we want to talk to you a minute."

The way his mother's eyes twinkled with delight, Jess wondered what the heck the woman was thinking.

Alice turned and opened the fridge door, pulling out the milk. "What's this about?"

Carson gestured toward the kitchen table. "Maybe we should sit down."

His mother's expression shifted, a flash of worry crossing her features before she carefully schooled them back to neutral. "Is something wrong?"

"No, not wrong," Jess said quickly, following Carson to the table. "It's just… important."

Once they were seated, Carson took a steadying breath. He'd rehearsed this moment in his head a dozen times since discovering the truth, but now that the moment had arrived, the words refused to come easily. "Mom," he began, his voice a little tighter than usual, "there's something you should know about Colton."

Alice's eyes moved between them as she slowly stirred the sugar and milk in her mug of tea.

"Colton is my son," the words rushed out before he could over think them again.

For a moment, the kitchen was so quiet Jess could hear

the wall clock ticking. Alice's face remained perfectly still, her eyes fixed on Carson's. Then a slow smile began to spread across her face. "I know."

Carson blinked. "You… what?"

"Of course I know," Alice's smile was now full and bright. "I suspected it the moment I saw him. Those dimples when he smiles—they're exactly like yours were at his age. And the way he concentrates when he's drawing? That's you all over again."

Jess couldn't help the small laugh that bubbled forth. "I should have known you'd figure it out."

"A mother knows her children," Alice reached across the table to take Carson's hand. "And their children." She turned to Jess, her expression more serious. "What I don't understand is why I'm only meeting my grandson now."

Carson opened his mouth to respond, but Jess gently touched his arm. "That's on me. I didn't know Carson was Colton's father until very recently. I mad inaccurate assumptions and married another man."

Alice nodded slowly. "And this other man raised Colton?"

"In a manner of speaking," Jess tried to keep the edge from her voice. "Todd wasn't much of a father. When he got sick and I had Colton tested, that's when I discovered the truth."

"And you came straight here," Alice finished for her, approval warming her voice. "That was the right thing to do."

Carson cleared his throat. "I'm sorry things weren't different. I just wish we hadn't lost all those years."

Alice's brow furrowed. "You know what I always say."

"If wishes were horses, beggars would ride," Carson recited easily.

"That's right," his mother nodded. "There's no point living in the land of coulda shoulda woulda. What matters is that you both know now, and you're doing the right thing." She turned to Jess, her eyes bright with unshed tears. "Thank you for bringing my grandson to us."

Jess felt her own eyes misting. "I'm sorry it took so long."

"We can't change the past," Alice reached for Jess's hand with her free one, still holding on to her son with the other hand. "But we can make the most of the future." She squeezed their hands, a mischievous glint appearing in her eyes. "And I have to say, you two being together makes perfect sense."

Carson shot Jess a quick glance. "Mom, we're not—"

"I know, I know," Alice said, waving away his protest. "You're just old friends reconnecting. But a mother can hope, can't she?"

The back door swung open before Carson could respond, and Colton bounded in, his face flushed with excitement.

"Mom! Carson! I helped groom Pepper and checked all her hooves! Clint says I'm a natural!"

Alice beamed at the boy. "Did he now? Well, Clint knows what he's talking about."

The way the kid grinned from ear to ear, as proud as an Olympic gold medalist, the family scene could have been a Norman Rockwell picture. She couldn't help but wonder how different their lives would have been if she'd just listened to her heart.

CHAPTER ELEVEN

Leaning against one of the porch posts, Carson's gaze followed Colton as he ran around with Brady in the yard. The German Shepherd was remarkably patient, trotting beside the boy and occasionally pausing to let Colton catch up. In the distance, Samson watched from his pen, not yet comfortable enough to join the play but clearly interested.

"He's really settled in quickly." Carson commented softly his gaze remaining on his son. His son. Would he ever get used to those words? "Acts like he's lived here his whole life."

"I know." Jess settled into one of the rocking chairs. "It's remarkable, honestly. The change in him since we've been here…"

Carson nodded, knowing exactly what she meant. The boy who'd been quiet and focused on his drawing pad back in the café had blossomed into an exuberant, curious kid who seemed determined to absorb every aspect of ranch life. Of course, the argument could be made that ranch life ran in his blood. Two hundred years of Sweets and now Colton would be the first of the next generation.

"I've been thinking about what you said before." Like he'd been doing, Jess's gaze remained fixed on her son.

"About?" Carson kept his voice even, matter-of-fact, hoping she was thinking about marrying him and in a favorable way.

"Getting married. To help the ranch." She gestured in her son's direction. "And Colton."

The kid was intent on teaching Brady how to sit on command. The dog, who'd known the command for years, played along patiently.

"He looks so happy, I can't decide if it would be right or wrong to keep him here, letting him think this is his home."

"Whether we do this or not, the Sweet Ranch will always be his home. His land. His roots."

"I know," she sighed, "but it's still not the same as thinking this is where you belong, and then when our deal ends, he'll be uprooted again."

Carson took a deep breath. He'd asked himself the same question more than once and didn't have any more answers than Jess. All he knew was that he didn't want to make a mistake. "I've been thinking too. What do you think if we build you and Colton a house here on Sweet Land?

Her head tipped to one side. "I'm not sure I'm following. You mean wait to marry till there's a house built?"

"No." He ran his hand across the back of his neck. He was going to botch this whole thing before it had even begun. "I mean we'll pick out a spot. Tell Colton it's going to be his new home soon. It will take time, especially since there isn't much money for material right now, but when we do, then you and Colton can move in."

"Without you?"

This was the part he hated, finally getting the one woman he'd always wanted, and then having to let her go. "Yes. Maybe, if he's still here on the ranch, still near all of us, the separation, the divorce, won't be as hard to handle." He didn't dare think about how hard it would be for him to have Jess around for years to come and have to pretend he didn't care.

"And if the ranch isn't on its feet in a year? If the house isn't built? What happens then?"

"I can go away for a while. I travel a lot. Our developments aren't always in this part of Texas. As a matter of fact, at some point when we can afford ranch hands again, or when that blasted lawsuit is settled, whichever comes first, I'll have to do some traveling anyway. It will seem normal to Colton."

"Normal," she muttered softly.

"Probably a poor choice of words."

She almost laughed at him. "Yeah, nothing about any of this is normal."

"I'm sorry." He really was. About a lot of things. Starting with not having fought harder for her when he knew Todd was bad news.

"Hey," she pushed to her feet and came over to his side, her hand on his forearm. "None of this is your fault. Not your dad, not Ray, not the mess I made of my life. None of it."

"Part of me knows that, but part of me can't help thinking if only…"

Her hand squeezed his arm. "My mother used to say, if my mother had wheels she'd be a car."

That made him smile. "Our moms would have been good friends."

"I think so." Jess took a step back. "What about telling him you're his father?"

Carson considered his words carefully. "One step at a time. As he gets used to me I'd like to believe, we'll know the right moment to tell him."

She nodded, her eyes following Colton as he ran across the yard, Brady loping beside him. Samson slowly inching closer to the fun. The boy's laughter carried to them on the evening breeze.

"I used to worry so much about him," she said softly. "That he wasn't getting what he needed. That he wasn't happy enough."

"And now?"

"Now look at him." Her voice caught slightly. "He's thriving here."

A comfortable silence settled between them, broken only by the distant sound of Colton's play.

Finally, Jess took a deep breath. "This may be the dumbest thing I've ever done," she said, a wry smile tugging at her lips. "Well, maybe marrying Todd can't be beat for the dumbest, but this may take second place. Let's do it."

Carson hoped his surprise wasn't showing. He honestly thought deep down she was going to tell him to go to hell in a hand basket for even thinking of such a ridiculous idea. "You're sure?"

"No," she laughed lightly. "I'm not sure at all. But sometimes the most ridiculous plans make the most sense."

"I guess ridiculous does pretty much cover it." Carson moved to her side, lightly touching her hand. "Whatever happens, we'll make sure Colton's happy. That's what matters most to both of us."

She nodded, their eyes meeting briefly before they both turned back to watch Colton, who had found a stick and was throwing it for Brady to fetch. Another trick the dog let him believe he'd only just learned. Then, to Carson's surprise, Brady dropped the stick in front of Samson and slowly the stressed dog sniffed the stick, looked at Brady, and Carson would have sworn Brady nodded at his new friend. Just as slowly, Samson picked up the stick, inched in Colton's direction, and dropped the stick in front of the boy's feet.

"Wow. I guess miracles do happen." Carson hoped that there was one more miracle in God's pocket for them.

If only time could stand still. At this moment, Jess couldn't remember feeling more relaxed, content, and more importantly, at peace.

"So," Carson said after a moment, "You up to telling Mom? I don't want to rush you, but, time is critical."

"I know."

"One other thing." He took hold of her hand and threaded their fingers together. "If we're going to pull this off, Mom has to believe it's for real. Holding hands will do a lot to help."

"Of course." Her gaze dropped to their laced fingers. So many memories flooded her thoughts. Happy memories. Good memories. She'd been so worried about Colton's well-being when this little charade was over, she hadn't really given any thought to her own. Giving his hand a tug and offering a weak smile, she sucked in a deep breath. "Time to go from the frying pan into the fire."

Almost holding her breath as she crossed the threshold, and noticed Alice elbow deep in bread dough, looking totally content in her element. Her future—and temporary—mother-in-law glanced up as they came in, a warm smile spreading across her face.

"Well, now, you two look like you've been hatching a plan." Her gaze dropped to their joined hands, and her smile widened.

"Actually, yes." Carson cleared his throat. "We've been talking, and… well…"

Jess could feel Carson's discomfort even if she weren't holding his hand. Gazing at him with a hint of a smile, she squeezed his hand, hoping to silently convey, you've got this.

With a slight nod of his head, Carson squeezed her hand back. "We're getting married."

Alice's hands stilled in the dough. For a moment, she said nothing, just stared at them. Then she let out a whoop of joy so loud that Jess half expected the roof to come off the house. "I knew it!" Alice beamed, wiping her hands on her apron. "The minute I saw you two together, I said to myself, 'Alice Sweet, those two belong together.' I'm just glad you didn't waste any time figuring it out for yourselves."

"It's not really quickly." Carson stared down at her and for a split moment, Jess thought she saw true love gazing down at her. Dang this man could act. "You might say it's been a decade in the making."

"That's right." Jess smiled at Alice. "Which is why we don't see any point in wasting time with a long engagement."

Immediately Alice's gaze dropped to Jess's left hand, then lifted to meet her son's.

"I, uh, wasn't prepared for her to say yes." Carson heaved a shoulder in an apologetic shrug.

Again, Jess squeezed his hand and took a chance

looking up at him and smiling. Maybe his mother would buy this charade.

"Anyhow," Carson let go of her hand and casually slid his arm around her waist, "we're thinking about getting married sooner rather than later."

"Sooner? How much sooner?" Alice had forgotten her dough.

Carson looked at Jess. "We thought we'd stop by the courthouse tomorrow and get the license, then after the waiting period, tie the knot."

"That's right." Jess figured she should corroborate his plans. "Small ceremony, just the family."

Alice's face fell. "You can't be serious. Not again."

Jess felt a pang of guilt at the disappointment on Alice's face. The woman had just learned she had a grandson; now she was being denied the chance to see her son properly married.

"No." Alice shook her head. "I don't know what's gotten into my children, but weddings should be in church, with flowers, and music, and friends, and then a party to remember for years to come."

"Mom," Carson's tone held a gentle warning. "This isn't exactly normal circumstances."

He certainly was right about that.

"Poppycock. A wedding is a wedding." Alice moved to the sink to wash her hands and heaved a sigh. "Okay." She nodded, reached for a towel to dry her hands and turned to face them. "Okay. I'll agree to fast. But we talk to Pastor John and have a church wedding, and then…"

"Mom," Carson almost whined.

"Under the circumstances, ma'am," Jess searched for just the right words. "I would feel more comfortable just having a quick ceremony at the courthouse."

She could see Alice fighting her own objections, then a smile stretched across her face and her eyes lit up. Jess didn't know if this was a good or bad thing.

"Here's what we're going to do." Alice tossed the dish towel aside and placing a moist towel over the dough, grabbed a pad and paper from the kitchen drawer. "We'll have a small wedding in the park. At the gazebo." She glanced up at them, with a pointed glare. "No church." Then she returned to her pad, scribbling who knew what when she spun around and enthusiastically waved her pen at them. "I've got it."

Carson's attention shifted from his mother to Jess and then briefly glancing out the window to see what Colton was up to, turned back to his mother. "You've got what?"

"The timing is perfect. We're having that barn dance this Saturday to raise money for the Flannagans after their barn burned down last month."

"Say again?" Carson didn't let go of her hand.

"The whole town is planning on coming anyhow, so you can get your license, have the small ceremony in the park and then the fundraiser party here at the ranch. We'll kill two birds with one stone. Besides, with everyone in a good mood, we might raise more money for the Flannagans."

There was nothing either of them could say. Alice was off calling her sisters, rambling about details, arrangements, flowers and even though Jess hadn't known the woman long, it was obvious to any idiot that there was no fighting Alice Sweet.

Jess felt Carson's arm tighten slightly around her waist. The gesture probably meant for show, offered comfort as well.

"You okay?" he asked softly, not that his mother would hear with her exuberant conversation in the other room.

She nodded. Her stomach twisted and she swallowed hard. Five more days and she would marry Carson Sweet. Not what she'd expected when she put Colton in the car and started driving west. She couldn't help but wonder what other surprises might be in store for her.

CHAPTER TWELVE

"**D**o you Carson Sweet take this woman to be your lawfully wedded wife, to have and to hold, from this day forward till death do you part?" Judge Earl stood on the steps of the Sweet Ranch back porch facing the Texas horizon.

"I do." Given the hurricane of emotions swirling.inside him, Carson's voice came out steadier than he would have expected.

The judge nodded approvingly. It had taken a bit of fancy footwork, but somehow they convinced the old geezer that saying love and obey was archaic. The only thing that convinced him was the concept that if they weren't planning on loving, why bother marrying. The till death do you part was a lost cause, but an acceptable compromise. Now, he turned to Jess. "And do you Jessica Pratt take this man to be your lawfully wedded husband, to have and to hold, from this day forward till death do you part?"

"I do." Jess's green eyes locked with his, a small smile playing at her lips.

"Then by the power vested in me by the great state of Texas, I now pronounce you husband and wife. You may kiss your bride."

Carson leaned forward, gently cupping Jess's face with one hand. This was the moment he'd been rehearsing in his mind. Not too brief to look uncommitted, not too passionate to embarrass his mother or Colton. As his dipped and his lips met Jess's, he was surprised by the warmth that flooded through him and the memories that flooded his mind from all those years ago. For a brief moment, the charade fell away, and it was just the two of them, as it should have been since all those years ago.

The small gathering of family at the porch steps erupted in applause, pulling him back to reality. He reluctantly broke the kiss, his hand sliding down to clasp Jess's.

Five days had passed in a whirlwind of preparations, yet somehow they'd managed to keep it relatively simple. His Texas tuxedo—pressed jeans, shined cowboy boots, crisp white shirt, and jacket—had been the perfect compromise between casual and formal. Jess looked stunning in a simple ivory dress with boots that his sisters had bulldozed her into buying during an impromptu shopping trip to Butler Springs. He'd been rather pleased that Jillian and NAME had been doing their best to let Jess know how much they appreciated having her as a new sister, even if only temporarily.

Carson glanced at the small assembly of family standing on and around the porch steps. His mother was dabbing at her eyes with a handkerchief, while his aunts Vicki and Liz beamed with approval. Garret, Rachel, and Jillian looked on with knowing smiles—they, of course, understood the real arrangement, though Carson had caught each of them watching him with curious expressions throughout the ceremony. Preston and Sarah stood closest to them, having been through this exact scenario themselves. Sarah gave Jess an encouraging wink.

But it was Colton who stole the show, proudly standing at Carson's side in his brand-new cowboy boots, jeans, and a miniature version of Carson's jacket. At first, he and Jess had been concerned how Colton would take the news that they were marrying. To their utter surprise, there wasn't a hint of concern or unhappiness in the child. Instead, they were confronted with a kid bouncing with joy at the prospect of getting to leave near the horses and the dogs. Going shopping for his first pair of real cowboy boots—like the grown Sweet men—had been the icing on the cake. Who knew it would be so easy? He only hoped, when the charade came to an end, and only Colton and his mother moved into the new house, that Colton would take that change in stride as well.

"Ladies and gentlemen," the judge announced, "I present to you, for the first time in public, Mr. and Mrs. Carson Sweet."

More applause and Carson felt Jess's hand tighten in his. When he glanced down at her, he saw a mix of emotions in her eyes that he couldn't quite decipher. Relief? Anxiety? Something else entirely? "You okay?" he whispered.

She nodded, her smile brightening. "Just taking it all in."

It had been a small victory, talking his mother out of the town park ceremony she'd initially envisioned. Alice had been determined to make this a community event, but Carson had insisted that the ranch, with the Texas landscape stretching endlessly behind them, was more appropriate for a Sweet wedding, and a more appropriate welcoming to the family for Jess. His mother had finally relented when Jess mentioned how much it would mean to her to be married in what was now her home.

Colton tugged at Carson's sleeve. "Does this mean you're my step-dad now?"

The innocent question landed like a punch to the gut. They still hadn't told him the truth. Carson knelt down to the boy's level, meeting those eyes that were so like Jess's.

"It means we're a family now," he said carefully. "That okay with you?"

Colton nodded enthusiastically. "Yeah! Brady and Samson are gonna be so excited!" Almost tripping over his new boots, Colton sprinted down the steps and headed for the two dogs, seated at the far edge of the barn.

Carson couldn't help but laugh. Leave it to a little boy to think about how the dogs would feel about the new family arrangement.

"Carson Sweet," his mother called, waving her camera. "Don't you dare move. I want a picture of the two of you right there on the steps."

He stood, placing one arm around Jess. The weight of the moment wasn't lost on him. This was his wife now, at least in the eyes of the law, his family, and his son. The feeling weighed on him more heavily than expected. A tinge of regret and sadness fell over him, almost wishing it weren't just for show. Then again, if wishes were horses....

"Everyone say 'Sweet'!" his mother called from several yards away.

With the ease of a person who had been corralling wayward children and extended family for years, his mom managed to get Colton back on the porch for an immediate family photo, as well as ones of the siblings, then the siblings and new members of the family, and handing the camera off to the judge, a few photos with her.

When he and she posed alone, she leaned into him. "I wish your father could be here." Before he could say a word, she patted his arm. "Oh, I know he's here in spirit, but…"

"I know Mom. I know." And just like that, he was reminded of why he and his siblings were going through so much to save the ranch that mattered so much to the entire Sweet family.

As soon as the photographs were taken, his mother herded everyone toward the barn. Everyone separated, buzzing about, making sure the food was out and ready, and the drinks cool and handy. The band members already in place were fine-tuning their instruments and tinkering with the equipment. His mother had made sure this would be the barnyard party of the century. Looking for his new bride, crossing the portable dance floor with a massive basket of sweet rolls, he could hear the roar of engines pulling onto the property. Any minute now they'd be flooded with half the town, heck, maybe all of it with his mother and aunts in charge. Lord how he hoped her heart wouldn't break at the end of the year.

Music spilled from the hay barn doors as dusk settled across the ranch. Jess sipped her punch, watching the sea of people crowding the makeshift dance floor and gathering around tables laden with food that seemed to multiply every time she looked.

The whole town had turned out—for the Flannagans, yes, but also for them. She'd lost count of how many hands she'd shaken, how many congratulations she'd received. Women she'd never met had hugged her like old friends, men had tipped their hats with respectful nods, and a parade of children had asked Colton if he was going to stay for good.

"There you are." Carson appeared beside her, two plates balanced in his hands. "Mom says you haven't eaten anything since breakfast, and I quote, 'That's no way for a bride to start her married life.'"

Jess laughed, taking one of the plates. "Your mother is something else."

"That she is." Carson's gaze drifted to where Alice showed Colton how to do the Texas Two-Step, both of them laughing as Colton's new boots slid on the polished floor. "Having second thoughts yet?"

"About our arrangement or the party?"

"Either. Both." He stabbed at a slice of brisket.

Shaking her head, the honesty of her answer surprised her. "Neither, actually. I keep waiting for the panic to set in, but so far..." She shrugged, taking a bite of potato salad.

"Well, the night is young." Carson winked at her, and Jess felt a flutter in her stomach that had nothing to do with hunger.

"So who's next?" Jess tracked his sisters fluttering around the barn, chatting with what Jess assumed were single men, then again, maybe they were just being friendly. There seemed to be a lot of that going around tonight.

Carson lifted his gaze in search of his siblings, then balancing his plate on his knees, blew out a sigh. "I honestly don't know. It's not easy finding people who have a reason to go along with our cockeyed plan."

"It's not cockeyed. A little unorthodox perhaps, but it comes from love."

The way Carson's eyes bore through her, for a moment, she'd have sworn he was trying to read her mind, or perhaps her soul. "Thank you for understanding."

Her head bobbed and she wished she better understood all the emotions tumbling around inside her as well as she understood how much Alice Sweets children had to love her to go through all this to save the ranch, yes, but more so, to save their mother.

"Most folks," Carson continued, "wouldn't understand how crushing it would be for Mom to lose the family ranch. She'd feel she let Dad down and that guilt would haunt her till the day she died." Now his gaze was focused on his mother chatting up a woman who sparkled so much if they hung her from the ceiling she'd make a great disco ball.

"Who is that?"

Carson followed her gaze and chuckled. "That's Mildred McEntire. The bling queen of West Texas, unofficially, of course."

"Of course," Jess chuckled alongside him.

For the next few minutes, Carson pointed out a few other town characters. "That over there, is Iris Hathaway. If you want news spread faster than wild fire, or the associated press, she's the one to talk to. If you have something to hide, better steer clear of her. That woman could get a rock to spill the beans."

Jess laughed a little harder. "I'll remember that."

The dance floor cleared and as the next song started, folks began filing onto the floor, lined up in multiple rows. The lively tune had people stepping and turning in surprised synchronization.

Setting his plate aside, Carson stood and extended his hand. "Shall we?"

"That depends on how badly do you want me to make a fool of myself."

"Not possible." His hand remained fixed, his smile so genuine, so warm, that Jess found herself placing her hand in his before she could think of another excuse.

The dance was simpler than it looked—lots of stomping, turning, and clapping that had everyone laughing rather than worrying about precision. Jess did her best to keep up. At one point she was supposed to turn left and spun in the wrong direction, crashing into Carson. His strong hands grabbed her arms before she could tumble backward. For just a split second, everything in the world felt oddly right.

The music shifted to something slower, couples began pairing off, and Carson's hands settled naturally at her waist.

"Our first dance as husband and wife," Carson said softly. "We should make it look good."

"For appearances' sake," Jess agreed, though the warmth of his hands through the fabric of her dress made it hard to remember this was all for show.

They swayed together, the space between them gradually shrinking until Jess could feel the steady beat of Carson's heart against her own. It felt natural, comfortable in a way she hadn't expected. In a way that brought memories crashing back of so many years ago. A time when she'd had hope that things were going to be better. That same feeling had returned in full force. And just like before, Carson Sweet was at the root of it all. When she looked up, she found Carson watching her with an intensity that made her breath catch.

"What?" she asked.

"Nothing." He smiled, but there was something in his eyes she couldn't quite read. "Just enjoying the moment."

She couldn't help but wonder if Carson's thoughts were also taking him back to another place and time.

As the night wore on and the party showed no signs of winding down, Jess found herself relaxing into this new reality. The friendly hugs, and echoes of congratulations, continued at every turn. Folks finally began to slowly slip away. At first folks with young children, then some of the older neighbors. Finally, with only close friends and family left, the band played the last song, and clean up began.

In the far corner, Colton had fallen fast asleep, curled up around Brady.

"How long do you think he's been there?" Carson asked.

Jess shrugged. "No idea, but the kid did party hard."

"He was a bigger hit than the bride and groom."

"Okay you two," Alice came up beside them. "Go put your son to bed. We'll finish cleaning up."

"We'll be back to help." Carson took a step in retreat.

"No." His mother turned to face him. "No bride and groom clean up after the party, they go on a honeymoon. And since y'all aren't taking a honeymoon, you can at least go enjoy the rest of your night. Alone."

Jess was pretty sure her cheeks were flushing bright red. Alice's implication was quite clear.

"Well, uh," Carson cleared his throat. "I'll get Colton."

Even as a toddler, Todd had never carried Colton with such ease and caring as Carson did from the back barn all the way to the house, up the stairs, and then into his new room. She reached for one boot and Carson the other. While she went to retrieve her son's pajamas, Carson tugged off the boy's jeans. They worked in surprising unison as if they had been tucking in a sleepy child all of his life.

How could that be? How is that they slid into the parenting role so flawlessly? Could anticipate the other's move, need? Was this a magical byproduct that came with all marriage licenses?

With Colton changed and tucked in, they each gave him a gentle kiss on the cheek and turned, gently latching the door closed behind them. Slightly down the hall was the master bedroom. The one that had been Alice and Charlie Sweets, then Preston and Sarah's, and now, her and Carson's. Oh, boy. Now what?

"I uh," Carson stood just inside the doorway. "Spoke with Preston and Sarah. They said that, the king-size bed made sleeping arrangements pretty simple." He shuffled to one side. "If you, uh, would like, I could, you know, put a bunch of pillows or something down the middle."

"Like in that old movie?"

"What?"

"Never mind."

"I'm sure there are extra pillows in the linen closet." He spun around. "I'll be right back."

She grabbed hold of his arm. "That's okay. I'm sure

we'll be fine. I sleep in one spot." No point mentioning Todd liked his space and she'd learned to not inch over or accidentally bumping Todd wasn't much different from waking a sleeping bear.

"Yeah, well, so do I." His gaze slid from her eyes to her lips and then back. Clearing his throat, his hand reached for hers.

For just a moment, she thought he was going to propose a totally different arrangement. And for another moment, her heart racing, she considered what the heck would she do. Except the decision was made for her when Carson leaned over, kissed her gently on the cheek, and softly uttered, "Thank you."

Nodding, she somehow managed to spit out the same. "Thank you for giving our son a brighter future."

He nodded, let go of her hand, and took a step back. "You can have the bathroom first. I'm going to go get a little fresh air. I won't be long."

Standing in place, she watched his back leave and once again wished she hadn't been such a fool all those years ago.

CHAPTER THIRTEEN

Carson squinted against the morning sun, watching the small moving truck rumble up the drive. He'd hoped the truck would be here before the wedding, but the day after was better than not at all. For the tenth time that morning, he wondered if he'd made a mistake. The plan had seemed perfect when he'd first spotted the forwarded notice from the Dallas Courts system tucked in with the other mail. He hadn't opened it—he'd never invade Jess's privacy like that—but the return address and official seal told him enough. That, combined with her casual mention of month-to-month rent and the obvious financial strain she was under, hadn't taken much to piece together.

A quick call to his cousin Declan and within hours, his suspicions had been confirmed. It had taken a bit more finagling to locate the name and phone number of the one neighbor Jess spoke of fondly. In exchange for paying the back rent, the landlord had agreed to allow the neighbor to box up all the belongings in the tiny apartment.

The truck came to a stop in front of the house, and Carson took a deep breath before heading down the porch steps. A skinny man in his forties hopped out of the driver's side, clipboard in hand. "Mr. Sweet?" The driver extended his hand. "I'm Dan. Got a delivery for you from Dallas."

"Thanks," Carson shook the man's hand. And once again, he wondered if he should have said something last night while he tried hard not to toss and turn and ignore the beautiful woman sleeping a few feet away from him.

The screen door swung open, and Carson turned to see Colton bounding out, followed by a curious-looking Jess. The driver lifted the tail gate and Jess's gaze settled on an old sofa. "That looks like mine."

Carson nodded.

Jess's hand flew to her mouth, her eyes widening as she stared at the contents of the truck. "How did you…? When did you…?"

"I saw the court notice in the mail," he admitted. "I didn't open it, but I had Declan confirm a hunch. Mrs. Kellerman agreed to help pack it all up. She insisted on making sure that the movers didn't pack and take trash."

Jess chuckled. "Yes, apparently when her sister moved to Dallas from New York, the movers took the trash bags out of the cans and packed it in boxes."

"I heard." He hesitated, studying her expression. "I hope you're not mad."

For a moment, Jess said nothing, her gaze moving from the truck to Carson and back again. "I honestly don't know what I feel right now, but no, mad isn't it."

Colton, who had been watching the exchange with wide eyes, suddenly darted forward. "Is my dinosaur collection in there? And my books? And what about—"

"Easy, buddy," Carson laughed, ruffling the boy's hair. "Let's start unloading and see what we've got."

To Carson's immense relief, she stood on her tippy toes and gave him a tender kiss on the cheek. "I had decided that what mattered most had come with me to the ranch, Colton, but apparently, he has other ideas. Thank you."

Another man who had climbed out of the passenger seat, held a small box. "Where do you want these?"

"For now, just set it all on the front porch. We'll sort it out."

"Look at this." Jess stared down at the first box labeled. Kitchen drawers. "Mrs. Kellerman labeled the boxes."

"I figure the stuff that will fit in the new house can be stored in the loft. Things you really don't want can be trashed or donated, and things y'all will need now can be brought into the house."

Jess nodded her agreement. "Okay. That," she pointed to a recliner that had seen better days, "can be kindling."

Laughing loudly, Carson nodded. "Works for me."

She proceeded to read every box before directing the driver whether to put it on the porch or to the side.

"It's here." Garret came out, a hot mug in hand. His gaze looked over his brother from head to toe. "And you're still alive so I guess you didn't screw up."

"He did not." Jess smiled up at his brother. "I think it was very thoughtful of him."

Garret grinned. "Yeah, that's my thoughtful brother." Setting his mug to once side, every time Jess said house, Garret lugged a box inside.

By the time the entire truck was emptied, all the siblings were moving items around like ants protecting the queen. A pile of furniture sat on one side of the porch to be donated, on the other side she places bed frames and dressers that still had plenty of use in them to be stored in the loft. The trash items were tossed in the back of the ranch pick up to be hauled to the dump.

Colton found the box labeled *toys* and within minutes had his new grandmother lugging the box inside and stabbing at it with a knife. Carson had to chuckle at the memory of the family at the breakfast table and Colton carefully broaching the subject of names. He had logically concluded that if his mother and Carson were married, then that meant Alice was sort of a grandmother. His mother had proudly announced she wasn't sort of a grandmother, she was now his official grandmother. Another few moments and they'd settled on her new name was Nonnie. All in all, by the end of the morning the front porch looked like a warehouse.

"I found it!" Colton's triumphant voice rang out from the other side of the room, where he and Nonnie were digging through the box of toys. He emerged holding a plush Tyrannosaurus rex, its fabric worn from years of love. "Rex is here!"

"I thought we'd lost him forever. I've actually tried finding another one online, but no glory." Jess smiled at her son's delight. "Guess I can cross that off my to-do list." She glanced up at Carson, "Thank you again."

"Thank you for not handing my head to me on a silver platter."

She took hold of his hand, squeezed it, and softly said, "Never."

If Carson could stand here, in this spot, with his wife and son smiling so happily, for the rest of his life, he would never ask God for another thing. Too bad, if wishes were horses.

Jess couldn't stop staring at the boxes now piled on the living room floor. Her entire life in Dallas, packed up and delivered to her doorstep without her having to lift a finger. She knelt beside a box labeled "Photo Albums" in a hasty scrawl, carefully peeling back the tape.

She still couldn't believe Carson had done this. In one gesture, he'd saved memories she'd resigned herself to losing, treasures from Colton's childhood she thought were gone forever. More than that, he'd done it without being asked, seeing a need and filling it. "Oh my goodness," she lifted a padded light-blue photo album with a single baby photo on the cover from the box. "I haven't seen this in ages."

Carson immediately abandoned his organizational efforts and crossed to sit beside her. "What is it?"

"Colton's baby book." She opened it gently as if her world would crumble if anything happened, revealing a photo of a red-faced newborn swaddled in a hospital blanket. "Look how tiny he was."

Carson leaned in, his shoulder pressing against hers as he studied the photo. "He has the same serious expression he gets when he's drawing."

"He does, doesn't he?" Jess laughed, turning the page.

Another photo revealed a sour-faced infant, face scrunched, clearly about to let out a scream to wake the dead.

"Colton had colic. I spent a lot of nights pacing the floor with him. Mrs. Kellerman was the one who told me to put his tummy on my shoulder blade and that it would help with the discomfort. I finally found an infant gas medicine that seemed to help. Even though it was hard pacing every day and night with him, I'd do it all over again if I had to."

Carson stared at the photo, let his finger barely rub over it. "Didn't Todd help."

"Pfft," practically spitting the sound, she shook her head. "No. Todd wasn't into babies, and he had to work early. He needed his sleep."

"So did you." Carson kept his gaze on the photos.

He had no idea how much those three little words meant to her. For so long she had been solely responsible for everything, herself, her son, and Todd. She wouldn't have admitted it to anyone, not even herself, but she was tired. Bone weary, to the soul, tired.

For the next hour, they sat side by side, poring over albums and memory boxes. Jess shared stories of Colton's first steps, his obsession with dinosaurs that started at age three, his earliest drawings—stick figures that somehow already showed the promise of artistic talent to come. Carson listened intently, asking questions, occasionally reaching out to touch a photo or a memento as if trying to connect with the years he'd missed.

Colton drifted in and out of their reminiscing, sometimes pausing to explain a particular toy or drawing before darting off to play with other refound toys. Brady followed him dutifully, sniffing each new treasure with curious interest. Colton's new best friend.

It had only been a few weeks since she'd driven into Honeysuckle with no plan beyond telling Carson the truth about Colton. Now here she was, surrounded by the physical evidence of her old life, seamlessly integrating into her new one. And at the center of it all was Carson, steady and reliable, offering support she hadn't even known to ask for.

So this was what it felt like, she realized, to have someone truly have your back. To have a partner in all the ways that mattered, even if the foundation of their relationship was built on practicality rather than passion.

"Look what I found!" Colton's excited voice broke

through her reverie as he bounded back into the room, clutching a small wooden box. "My rock collection!" Apparently, he and Nonnie along with uncle Garret had been sorting through the boxes from Colon's old room, now piled in his new room.

He plopped down between them, carefully opening the box to reveal an assortment of stones in various shapes and colors. "This one glows in the dark," he explained, holding up a pale green rock. "And this one has real gold in it. See the sparkles?"

"That's amazing," Carson said with genuine interest. "I used to collect rocks when I was your age too."

"Really?" Colton's eyes widened. "Do you still have them?"

"I think they might be in a box in the attic." Carson glanced at Jess, a mischievous glint in his eye. "If I still have them, I bet Nonnie knows exactly where they are."

"Cool!" Colton turned and practically vibrating with excitement, bolted back up the stairs, calling Nonnie on his way.

"I don't know that I have ever seen him quite this happy, every single day."

"I'm glad." Carson's gaze returned to the last pages of another album. "Ones with Colton older, his first day of kindergarten, his last birthday, Christmas."

Carson flipped forward and back a few pages. "I don't see any of Todd. Not very photogenic?"

"Not very present." She didn't want to think about all the years with a good man she'd robbed her son of. "I should have left him years ago."

"Hey," Carson reached under her chin with one finger and turned her head to face him. "You did the best you could under difficult circumstances. The proof that it was more than good enough is in how happy and well-adjusted Colton is despite the man you thought was his father."

His smile was warm, genuine, and for a moment, Jess allowed herself to forget that this was all temporary, that in less than a year they'd be going their separate ways. For now, it was enough to be here, surrounded by the pieces of her past while building something new, however fleeting it might be.

Yes, Jess thought, watching Carson push to his feet and carry the box of memories upstairs to their room. Even if none of this would be forever, even if their budding relationship was built on convenience rather than love, what they had right now was real enough. And after everything they'd been through, maybe that was all that mattered.

CHAPTER FOURTEEN

Carson guided the Jeep over a rough patch of terrain, glancing in the rearview mirror at Colton, who bounced excitedly in the back seat. The boy had his backpack clutched to his chest, the binoculars and his prized telescope handed down from Carson safely at his side.

"How much farther?" Colton asked for at least the fifth time.

"About ten minutes," Carson answered with the same patience he'd shown the previous four times. "If the mustangs are still around, we might find them grazing just past that ridge."

"If they're not," Colton watched the horizon carefully, "can we go back to the canyon where we found them last time?"

"Maybe," Carson nodded. "But no promises. Fixing fence lines can go quickly or take a while. We'll have to play it by ear."

The kid started at him through the rearview mirror as if Carson had spoken in Greek.

"Playing by ear means you wait to see what happens and then make a decision."

An expression of understanding took over his son's face, and Colton nodded, his attention returning to the land in the distance. No doubt scanning for those wild horses.

They crossed into the northwestern section of the ranch, the landscape as flat and dusty ahead as it had been behind them. Carson pulled the Jeep to a stop near a fallen tree. "We'll park here. There's a section of fence several yards ahead that needs fixing. From there, we'll set up the telescope."

"You can draw or look for the horses. Whichever you prefer." Jess hopped out of the Jeep. "I'm going to help Carson with the fence. Or at least try to."

"You'll do fine. Mom used to work with Dad before any of us were born. The trick is to learn how to string barbed wire without losing a finger."

Jess gave him a look.

"Kidding," Carson said with a laugh. "Mostly."

They gathered their supplies—Carson's tools, a small cooler with lunch, and Colton's all-important optical equipment. The walk was pleasant, with Colton charging ahead then doubling back every few minutes to report on interesting rocks or lizards he'd spotted.

"There's the fence," Carson pointed to where a section had fallen, they suspected all of this recent damage was thanks to the newly migrated horses.

Colton immediately set up his position, unzipping his backpack, the binoculars around his neck, the telescope nearby. A deep frown for a young boy formed between his brows. "I don't see them."

"You keep watching," Carson smiled. "Give us a heads-up when you spot them."

For the next half hour, Carson showed Jess how to remove the damaged wire and string a new section. She was a quick learner, and he found himself enjoying her determination to master each task, but more than that, he simply enjoyed her company. Anyone would think that having to spend all day, every day, with a person would begin to wear thin, but so far, every minute of time with Jess had become very special to him.

"Out of curiosity," Jess, pulled her hand out of the glove and sucked on a pricked finger. "What happens if a ranch hand gets hurt out here in the middle of nowhere?"

"All ranch vehicles are a bit of a combination of tool shed and first aid station. Usually we have enough supplies nearby for a minor incident." He pulled her hand away from her mouth and looked at her finger. "Give me a second."

She stuck the finger back in her mouth.

"Here we go." From one of his sacks, he pulled out

some antiseptic ointment and a Band-Aid. "This will fix it up."

Her gaze softened as he tended to her finger. "Not bad for a real estate developer."

Carson smiled at her, wishing he didn't have to let go of her hand. "Once a rancher always a rancher. We all keep our hands in the family business, and deep down, we all love it at least a little."

Staring at her bandaged finger, she frowned. "What happens if someone is really hurt?"

His mind scurried back to when they'd found their mother trapped in the barbed wire not that many months ago. "We thank God for cell phones. Alert fellow hands. But in a pinch, there are line shacks scattered all over the property."

"Line shack?"

"Small cabins, really. The hands use them when they're working far out and need shelter from an unexpected turn of bad weather. Sometimes, a small injury might require holding up for a bit until help can come."

"Like ranger stations?" Jess wiped her forehead with her forearm.

"Exactly. There's one not far from here. When we finish up, I'll show you. Not that we expect to put you to work, but it doesn't hurt to know where they are in case of emergency."

The rest of the repair job went quickly. To Colton's chagrin, no horses appeared, but he had a great time drawing a bird that seemed to be delighted to stay perfectly still and pose for him. After a simple lunch of sandwiches and fruit, Carson drove them to a small, weathered cabin standing lonely in the middle of nowhere.

"This is one of the oldest ones." He shoved the door open wide. The cabin was simple—one room with a small wood stove, a basic twin bed hewn from ancient two-by-fours, some shelves with canned goods, an ancient table with two chairs, and a large mound dead center of the cabin with a dirty sheet tossed over it. "What the heck?"

"I'm guessing, this is not part of the standard stock?"

Jess moved to stand beside him.

"No." Pulling back the old sheet, he froze. "That son of a—" he caught himself, glancing at Colton. "This is impossible."

"What is it?" Jess grabbed hold of his arm.

"A hay baler. And not just any hay baler." Carson pulled the tarp away completely, revealing a gleaming piece of machinery. "This is one of the custom balers Dad ordered right before he died. We thought Ray had sold it off with the other equipment he stole."

"Could there have been a mistake?" Her hand on his arm, her voice came out very low.

Shaking his head, Carson's jaw tightened. "I don't have an explanation, but I'll come back with my brothers and the right transportation. We'll take this where it belongs." Heaving out a deep breath, he tried to wipe his concerns from his face and turned to his wife and son. "Come on. Let's go home and tell everyone what we've found."

The three left the shed, locking it up again, but something was definitely off, and whatever it was, Carson didn't like it one bit.

Since leaving Dallas, Jess didn't get very many texts, and almost forgot what her phone buzzing meant. Retrieving it from her pocket, she glanced down: *In thirty minutes, family meeting in dad's study.* Jess blinked. It took her a moment to realize she was now part of the Sweet family and hence, included in a group text about a family meeting.

Checking her watch, the phone buzzed again. *Don't tell Mom.* Okay, now she had to wonder what the heck was going on that Alice couldn't be included but she was. The least Jess could do was help make sure that Alice didn't stumble into the study. Waiting ten minutes, she went to the kitchen and finding Alice at the sink, headed for the cupboard.

"Did you enjoy this morning working on the fences?"

Alice stuck a clean dish in the nearby drain board.

"Very much." Pulling out a mug, she filled it with water and placed it in the microwave. "But I'm a bit worn out. Not to mention sore." That much was the truth. "Thought I'd make some warm tea and go lay down for a bit."

"Good idea. Naps always help right what's wrong."

Her gaze lifted to the kitchen window where Colton was in his usual place, playing in the dirt with both Brady and Samson at his side. "I know Colton is all right with the two dogs, but would you mind keeping an eye on him for me."

"Absolutely." Alice beamed. "I'll do better than that. We'll go check out the new foal in the barn."

"He'll love that."

Alice stood a little taller and grinned like a cat with a belly full of cream. "I know."

Carrying her tea in hand, Jess proceeded to the study where Rachel and Jillian were already seated.

Pouring herself a cool drink, Rachel glanced at Jess "Any idea what this is all about?"

"No." She shook her head, looking up when footsteps grew closer from the hallway.

Practically tip toeing into the room, Sarah, Preston's wife, inched to the nearest chair. "Just for the record, it is almost impossible to sneak quietly into a house wearing cowboy boots."

The two sisters chuckled.

"Alice is in the barn with Colton."

All three of the other women snapped around to face Jess.

She shrugged. "I thought it might be helpful to get her out of the house."

"Oh," Rachel collapsed into her favorite chair. "I gotta admit. My brothers do know how to pick good women." She raised her drink to Jess. "Thank you."

Another few minutes and the three brothers marched into the room. Carson headed straight for the bar, pouring three bourbons, handing one to Preston who went and sat on the arm of the chair where his wife sat, the next to Garret who took a seat at their father's desk, and taking the last one himself, he came and sat beside Jess on the small sofa.

"What's going on?" Rachel leaned forward.

Garret waved at Carson. "This is your discovery bro, the floor is yours."

"Bottom line, we have a problem."

Everyone waited quietly for his next words.

"This morning when Jess and I took Colton to go fix some downed fence line and search for the mustangs again, we stopped at the nearest line shack. Inside, I found the usual, and one of the hay balers Dad had bought."

"What?" Jillian leaned forward. "I thought Ray sold them all."

"So did we," Preston interjected.

"This afternoon Preston, Garret and I returned to the shack with the flatbed and whatever me might need to hoist it and bring it home. Figured we could either use it the way Dad had intended or sell it and pay off some of the loan."

Heads bobbed.

"Makes, sense," Rachel agreed.

"Except for one teeny-weeny little problem," Carson continued. "When we reached the shack, the baler was gone."

"What?" Rachel uncrossed her legs and sprang up. "What do you mean, gone?"

"Gone. G. O. N. E."

"But who?" Sarah asked this time, her hand tightly gripping her husband's.

"And that," Garret steepled his fingers in front of him, "is the sixty-four thousand dollar question."

"You don't think…" Rachel scanned the room, but didn't say another word.

Jess had watched the interaction amongst the siblings, recognized the growing concern, but had no clue what it all meant.

Carson reached over, taking Jess's hand in his and squeezed. "It could be any number of people. Could be rustlers, a burglary ring, or," Carson swallowed hard. "Ray and his men are still around."

Now she understood. Understood why Carson had

gripped her hand, why the others looked more nervous than a cat in a room full of rockers.

"So," Jillian didn't address anyone in particular, "what do we do? Call the sheriff?"

Carson shook his head. "He doesn't know anything more than we do. He's been unable to track down Ray or any of the others. If it's them, he doesn't know it."

"Maybe Clint?" Rachel asked. "I mean, I know he's been good to Mom, but then, we thought the same thing about Ray."

"No." Preston sighed. "He was in the barn with Colton all morning and then with Mom while we were off to the shed."

"What I want to know," Sarah asked, "is does anyone else think it rather a coincidence that one minute it's there and the very same day we find it, it's gone?"

"Wait," Jillian eyed her sister-in-law, "are you saying they were watched?"

Sarah shrugged. "No, but the timing of all this is rather uncanny."

"We thought the same thing." Carson continued to hold Jess's hand. "Now the question is, what do we do about it?"

"Can we trust Clint?" Rachel suggested.

All three brothers shrugged.

"Damn," Rachel muttered under her breath.

"That about covers it." Carson inched forward in his seat. "From now on, no one goes anywhere alone. And first thing in the morning we'll pair up and start checking out all the line shacks, just in case there's anything else hidden we might want to know about."

Preston spoke up, "We're also going to install cameras. If anyone besides us comes near the shacks, we'll know it."

"Don't you need wifi and power?" Jillian asked.

"No." Preston shook his head. "We can use batteries and SD cards."

"If you're going to secure the line shacks," Rachel stood up. "We should secure the house too. Cameras. Whatever. You know, just in case."

Again, all the men nodded, and Jess could feel a sense

of panic tickling her spine.

The conversation continued for a little bit longer, everyone more alert, Jillian and Rachel promising to carry again until this mystery was resolved.

When everyone left the room, Carson remained seated. Still holding on to her hand, he turned. "I know joining the family now is something like trial by fire, but I promise you, everything will be all right."

She nodded slightly.

"Do you trust me?"

It only took a second for her to nod again, barely surprised that she meant it.

"Good. Then we'll figure this out, and you have to know, everyone in this house will keep an eye out for Colton."

Not for a second had she doubted that. "Whatever the family needs, count on me." She just hoped she wasn't promising more than she could deliver.

CHAPTER FIFTEEN

"I don't know." Alice Sweet ran the hoof pick through the crevice of Blaze's front left hoof, carefully removing packed dirt and small stones. "All this sudden rush to install cameras everywhere. I don't think I like it."

"The world is changing." Clint had already removed the saddle and blanket, placing them over the tack room door. "Pretty soon there will be cameras tattooed to people's foreheads."

Her hands stilling, Alice glanced over at their only ranch hand before moving to Blaze's front right hoof. "So you don't think it's a big deal?"

"What I think doesn't matter."

"It does to me. You could have gone in with the others and been long gone by now, but you didn't. What do you think?"

Clint approached Blaze's head and gently stroked the horse's cheek before unbuckling the bridle, easing the bit from the animal's mouth. "Miss Sweet."

"Alice."

"Alice, I think as much as we'd all like to be living back in the days of Leave it to Beaver and the Brady Bunch, the world is changing and we have to change with it. If having a few cameras around the ranch makes your children happy, what does it hurt?"

It wasn't the cameras themselves that bothered her, it was the unexpected urgency that came with them. "I suppose." She moved to the horse's back hooves, continuing her methodical cleaning.

Hanging the bridle on a hook, Clint retrieved a comb

and brush from the grooming kit. Working the comb in circular motions along Blaze's dusty flanks, he loosened dirt and hair before following with the brush to sweep it away. His gaze seemed pensive, teetering on concern, but she couldn't be sure. The man had never been a fountain of conversation—or smiles. More than once she'd wondered what was the story behind the lone cowboy?

A week had gone by since they'd discovered the found and lost baler. Cameras had been installed, and even though the family had been split on whether or not to tell their mother the reason why, the nay side won the argument. Carson still wasn't totally comfortable with that decision, after all, his mother wasn't a feeble widow unable to deal with realty. Then again, she had a lot of stress on her plate and not adding one more thing to it seemed reasonable.

Rubbing the back of his neck, Carson stepped out of the barn, and his new habit had him carefully scanning the yard. The Texas sun had begun its slow descent, stretching long shadows across the dust-packed ground. No sign of intruders, or trouble, and no sign of Colton.

His son was always easy to spot—usually perched on the porch railing with his sketchbook balanced on his knees, or chasing Brady and Samson in wide circles around the yard, his laughter carrying across the property. But the yard was empty, not even the faithful dogs were about.

An odd feeling crept up his spine, and an uneasy feeling settled between his shoulder blades. Something wasn't right. He'd grown accustomed to the boy's presence, the way he filled spaces with energy and questions and constant motion. The stillness felt wrong.

"Probably inside with Mom," he muttered to himself, but even as he said it, the uneasiness grew.

Carson crossed the yard in long strides, taking the porch steps two at a time. The screen door creaked as he pulled it open and stepped into the cool dimness of the house.

"Colton?" His voice echoed in the entryway. No answer.

In the kitchen, Jess and his mother stood beside the counter, heads bent over a cookbook. His sister Jillian sat at the table peeling potatoes. The same table he'd expected—or hoped—to find Colton happily drawing.

Jess looked up, her smile blooming then instantly withering as she registered his expression. "What is it?"

"Have you seen Colton? He's not in the barn, not outside."

His mom straightened. "Isn't he was with you?"

"I haven't seen him since lunch," Carson replied, the weight in his stomach growing heavier.

"He's probably upstairs." Jess forced a smile that looked anything but relaxed.

"You're probably right." With Jess at his side, he strode to the bottom of the stairs and called upstairs. "Colton."

No response.

"Colton, honey," Jess called up the hall, her voice not quite as calm or confident as he'd like. "Are you upstairs?"

Wiping her hands on her apron, Alice came beside them, her movements quick and efficient. "I'll check the downstairs rooms."

"Maybe his door is closed and he can't hear us." Carson took the steps three at a time, calling Colton's name. The boy's bedroom door stood ajar. Carson pushed it open, scanning the space—unmade bed, toys scattered across the floor, drawings tacked to the walls. But no Colton.

His gaze caught on the empty hook by the door where the backpack usually hung. The binoculars that normally sat on the nightstand were gone too.

"Blast," he breathed, spinning on his heel and returning downstairs.

In the hallway, he nearly collided with Preston and Sarah.

"What's going on?" Preston asked. "We heard shouting."

"Can't find Colton." The words tasted bitter on his tongue.

Sarah's eyes widened. "Have you checked the barns? You know how he loves the horses."

"That's where I came from. Not there." A cold, heavy weight settled in Carson's stomach.

"He wouldn't leave the ranch alone, would he?" Jess leveled her gaze with his. "He knows better." The last words sounded like she was trying to convince herself rather than stating a fact.

Where could the kid be?

"He can't have gone far." Preston's words did little to erase the knots forming in Jess's stomach. Surely he wouldn't run off. This ranch was so large, it would be easy to get lost and take days to find him. No, she was not going to let her mind run away with. Colton was a good boy. He had to be somewhere. Somewhere near.

Garret burst through the door, "What's going on?"

"We can't find Colton," Sarah answered first.

Phone in hand, Garret began tapping. "Let me check the security cameras."

Of course. Jess's nerves eased slightly. That would let them see where Colton was.

As Garret pulled up the footage, Carson placed his hand firmly around Jess's waist. She'd never been so thankful for a man's support in her life. Her own hands felt clammy as she waited for a report on the footage.

Alice hovered behind her son, muttering prayers under her breath.

"There," Garret pointed. "Out the door, looks like a bit over a two hours ago."

Carson's grip on her waist tightened ever so slightly. She could feel his tension, coiled tight like a rope about to snap. How had she not noticed her son had been gone for over two whole hours?

On the small screen, they watched Colton ease down the rear steps, backpack slung over his shoulder, Brady trotting at his heels. The boy looked back once at the house, then squared his shoulders and set off with determined strides.

"Why would he run away?" Worry and disappointment mixed in her eyes.

Carson heaved a deep sigh. "There's no reason for him to run away. Where would he go? Why would he go?"

"The horses." Jess's fingers clenched at her side. "He's been talking about them all week, drawing them, asking when we could go back to the canyon."

"He took Brady," Alice said, touching Jess's arm. "That dog won't let anything happen to him."

Carson was already moving toward the door. "I'll take the Jeep. We can cover more ground faster."

"I'm coming with you," Jess didn't mean to snap.

Carson nodded once. "Preston and Sarah, Garret and Rachel—can you check the east and south sections, just in case? We'll head west, follow his trail."

"I'm coming too." Alice tossed the rag she'd still been holding to one side.

"No." Carson stepped away, closer to his mother. "Someone has to stay here in case he doubles back, let us know."

She could see the reluctance in his mom's face before, lips pressed tightly, she nodded. "Makes sense." Placing a hand on Carson and Preston's shoulders, she gave them a little shove. "Now go find my grandson."

CHAPTER SIXTEEN

The weight in Carson's stomach had transformed into a fierce, protective instinct that burned like fire. Colton was his son. His responsibility.

The Jeep bounced hard over the rough terrain, each jolt rattling Carson's teeth and doing nothing for his frayed nerves. He pushed the accelerator, demanding more speed even as the vehicle protested. Every second stretched into an eternity. If anything happened to Colton.

In his head, Carson envisioned every worst-case scenario. One after another bounced around in his vivid imagination. He could see Colton alone at the diminutive canyon floor, small and vulnerable against the towering ridge with no one to hear his calls for help. More frightening, a rattlesnake coiled in the shadows of a rock ready to pounce, its warning rattle drowned out by the wind. Would Colton even recognize the rattler's sound? Did city boys from Chicago know anything about venomous snakes? And what if Colton had fallen? Slipped on loose shale, tumbling down a steep incline, left lying injured on the hard ground with no way to get back to safety. More frightening than any of those extreme scenarios was the most likely danger—the mustangs—wild, powerful creatures startled by a boy's sudden appearance, their hooves thundering across the canyon floor with an unsuspecting Colton frozen, mesmerized, in their path.

No. He shut the thoughts down, clenching his jaw so tight his temples throbbed. He couldn't let his mind travel that road. Not now.

At his side, Jess checked her cell phone, waiting to hear from someone at the house with news that Colton had been found lost in his artwork, or asleep with Brady in an overlooked corner.

"Anything new?" Carson didn't look at her, his gaze remained fixed on the terrain ahead, for any sign of a little boy walking.

Jess shook her head. "If he's been walking for over two hours, how far can he have gone?"

"The canyon area is about five or so miles from the ranch. I'm no expert on nine-year-olds, but if he's running and playing around with Brady, he could be there already."

"How far away are we?"

"Almost there." One thing he tried to find comfort in was Brady. That dog was smart as a whip, well trained, fearless, and most importantly, loyal and devoted. Carson just prayed that dog kept his son safe until he got to him.

Not much time had passed when Jess pointed through the windshield. "There!" her voice tight with hope.

The canyon area that was barely much deeper than an oversized trench, came into view, a wide, sun-baked cut in the earth that sloped down into more dirt and dust. Carson scanned the area frantically. If Colton wasn't here, where could he be? Where should Carson look next?

Carson barely stopped the Jeep before he was out, boots hitting the dirt hard. Across the Jeep, Jess did the same, her eyes darting all around, she cupped her mouth, preparing to call out to her son.

"Don't." Carson grabbed her arm. "We don't want to spook the horses if they're down there.

"With Colton," she muttered softly.

All he did was nod. Taking hold of Jess's hand, the two of them hurried across the land to the canyon edge, scanning the distance his heart sank with no sign of Colton, only a herd of horses mulling about below, and then— movement caught his attention. A small figure crouched low against the darkening landscape. Brady's muscular form hovering protectively nearby, his stance alert, ears forward. The dog's attention was divided between the boy and the herd, his training evident in how he positioned himself.

It had to be Colton. Relief crashed through Carson like a wave, immediately followed by a fresh surge of adrenaline when he registered what he was seeing. The impact jarred his knees but he barely felt it, every sense focused on the scene unfolding fifty yards ahead. "Stay put," he quickly told Jess. "Keep the phone handy. We may need help—and fast."

Jess nodded, her gaze filled with worry and love, whether for him or their son, or both, he didn't know. So softly, he barely heard her, she whispered, "be careful."

Colton, crouched low, extended his small fingers toward a foal curled in the dust. The animal looked tiny, vulnerable—but its mother did not. The mare stood just a few feet away, muscles tensed beneath her dusty coat, ears pinned flat against her head.

Just what he didn't need. An angry mare in mama bear mode protecting her young. Colton, in his innocence, had gotten between them. Carson's heart slammed against his ribs.

"Colton." He kept his voice low, even, though everything in him screamed to yell *run*. Instead, as softly as he could and still be heard, he called to Colton, "Don't move."

The boy's head turned, just a fraction. Just enough to be considered a threat. Without hesitation, in a snap, the mare charged.

Carson lunged forward, covering the distance in three desperate strides. He grabbed Colton by the shoulders, swinging him behind his back in one fluid motion. A sharp, white-hot pain tore through his upper arm as the mare's hoof clipped him—hard.

He stumbled but held his ground, feeling Colton's small fingers digging into his waist.

The mare whipped around, front hooves pawing the air. Ready to strike again. A low, rumbling growl cut through the tension. Brady had circled around, placing himself between Carson's back and the angry mare, his body lowered into a defensive stance. The dog's military training had kicked in—he was now guarding both his charges, ready to engage if necessary.

Damn.

Gravel crunched under Jess's feet as she stood at the canyon's edge. Her heart hammered against her ribs, each beat painful. She wanted to scream, run, snatch Colton away, and Carson too. But she was frozen in place, too far away to do anyone any good. Not that she had any clue how to save the two people who meant most to her in the world. All she could do was watch the terrifying tableau before her—the man she loved, their son, and a furious wild horse with every protective instinct in her body fully engaged.

She had never been so scared in her life. Not when she'd learned the truth about Todd not being Colton's father, not when she'd faced eviction, not even when she'd first driven into Tuckers Bluff with no idea what awaited her. This was pure, primal fear that numbed her limbs and stole her breath.

Carson stood like a living shield between Colton and the wild mare, his posture tense but controlled. Her son—their son—pinned behind him, wide-eyed, clutching the back of Carson's shirt with white-knuckled fingers. Even from this distance, she saw the exact moment when Colton's expression shifted from childlike enchantment to gut-wrenching fear and it cut through her like a knife.

At Carson's side, Brady stood, hackles raised, a continuous low growl emanating from his throat. The dog's presence seemed to give Carson an advantage—the mare's attention now split between the man and the unfamiliar predator, but the dog's presence did nothing to alleviate the fear in Colton's eyes.

She needed to do something, anything. But if she made a mistake—if she startled the mare or distracted Carson at the wrong moment—it could be catastrophic. Carson could get trampled. Colton could get hurt. One wrong move and this already dangerous situation could turn deadly in an instant.

Slowly, a single measured step at a time, she inched closer, hugging the canyon's edge, desperate to help but not having a clue what to do. The distance seemed to stretch forever, each step taking too long. Finally, close enough to hear the mare's heavy breathing and Carson's low murmurs, she stopped. Her fingers dug into her palms, nails biting into sweaty flesh.

The animal reared up suddenly, powerful front hooves pawing at the air. Jess's heart stuttered to a near stop, a silent scream caught in her throat. This was it—the mare was going to strike. She was going to watch Carson get killed, while protecting their son.

When Carson stepped forward—intentionally moved toward the danger instead of away—with Colton still clinging to his back, she had to clasp her hands against her mouth to stop herself from screaming out loud. Every instinct in her body screamed that he was doing the wrong thing, that he should be backing away, running, anything but confronting the angry animal. But she had no other choice than to trust him, to trust that Carson knew what he was doing, that he would not only protect their son at any cost, but he would get them both out alive—he had to.

Praying silently, promising God anything and everything she could think of, she watched intently as the mare huffed, nostrils flaring, muscles bunched and ready to react. Carson lifted his hands slowly, palms out, making himself bigger without being threatening. His movements were so controlled, so deliberate, it almost felt like she was watching a dance. With uncanny precision, Brady mirrored his movements, neither advancing nor retreating, but maintaining his protective position. The retired military dog probably understood the delicate balance of this standoff better than most humans would.

He kept his voice low, the same tone she'd heard him use with spooked calves and nervous foals. "Easy now."

The mare's ears twitched—still alert but not completely flattened against her head. Jess had no idea if that was a good sign or bad sign. Her knowledge of horses was limited what little she'd learned at Colton's, but wild horses were completely outside her wheelhouse. All she knew was that the animal looked ready to charge again.

"Easy, mama," Carson murmured, taking another small step, angling slightly to the side. "We're not here to hurt your baby."

Frozen with fear, Jess was almost mesmerized watching Carson deal with the angry mare. Everything he did was slow, measured, controlled. Not backing down, but not challenging either. Just a steady, calm presence in the face of danger. In that moment, she saw him in a completely new light—not just as the man she'd begun to love all those years ago, who had married—for all intents and purposes—a near stranger to save his mother and their beloved family ranch, but someone with a quiet strength that ran bone-deep.

Jess prayed some more, her fingernails still biting into her palms, her heart barely beating as she watched the continued standoff. The mare huffed and stamped her hooves again, the sound like thunder in the quiet canyon. Jess held her breath, certain this couldn't be good. The massive animal looked unconvinced—but then she hesitated.

For an eternal moment, horse and man regarded each other, a silent communication that Jess couldn't interpret. Then—just like that—the mare turned. The massive animal wheeled around, dust kicking up behind her powerful hooves, and she bolted back to her foal and the rest of the herd. Unconvinced all was secure, Brady didn't relax his stance until the mare was a safe distance away, then the German Shepherd gave a single soft 'woof' as if signaling the all-clear. Only then did the dog turn his attention fully to Colton, nuzzling the boy's hand, sniffing from shoulder to shin, as if checking him for injuries.

Her nerves shattered like glass. Barely registering the rough terrain, Jess ran. Heat filled her lungs, tears streamed down her face. Her legs moved of their own accord, carrying her forward with desperate speed. She reached Colton first—pulling him away from Carson and into her arms, pressing her forehead to his, clutching him like she'd never let go.

His small body trembled against hers, his breath coming in hitching sobs. "Mom," he choked out, "I'm sorry, I'm so sorry."

"Shh, it's okay, you're safe now," she murmured into his hair, rocking him slightly, reassuring herself as much as him. Her gaze dropped to Brady dutifully at her son's side. Somehow she knew the dog would have given his life to protect her son from danger. "Good boy, Brady. Good boy."

Just a few feet away Carson stood there, breathing hard, one hand gripping the arm where the mare had struck him. Blood seeped between his fingers, staining his shirt sleeve a dark crimson. His face was pale beneath his tan, but his eyes—his eyes were fixed on them, filled with a fierce protectiveness that took her breath away. He'd saved their son.

Still holding Colton tightly against her, Jess met his gaze across the small distance. Something electric passed between them. And that was it. The moment she knew. The moment she understood, down to her bones, that she couldn't live without him.

CHAPTER SEVENTEEN

Jess held the passenger door open as Carson climbed out of his truck, wincing as his arm protested the movement. The drive back from Doc Conroy's office had been uncomfortable, each bump in the road sending a fresh jolt of pain through his shoulder. But he'd been right—no broken bones. Just a nasty bruise that stretched from his shoulder halfway down his bicep, already turning an impressive shade of purple.

The screen door creaked open and his mother appeared, her eyes scanning him from head to toe. "Well?" her voice rang out tight with concern.

"Clean bill of health." He managed a smile despite the throbbing. "Or at least as clean as you get when a horse tries to use you as a soccer ball."

She stepped aside to let him in, her hand automatically reaching for his good arm. "Sarah's father said it wasn't broken?"

"Not even cracked. Just looks worse than it is." He wasn't entirely sure that was true—it felt pretty damn bad—but he wasn't about to admit that.

Family filled the kitchen, everyone lingering around as if their presence would somehow speed his recovery. Preston leaned against the counter, beer in hand, while Garret sat at the table playing cards with Rachel. On the floor, Colton sat cross-legged, Brady's head resting in his lap, the boy's fingers absently stroking the dog's ears.

"You're lucky." Sarah came forward handing him a cool glass of sweet tea. "Another inch higher and that hoof would have done real damage."

"Your handiwork kept me from bleeding all over the

truck," Carson smiled at his sister-in-law. "Your dad said you did good, if you ever want to give up saving dogs, he's got room for you."

Sarah let out a loud burst of laughter. "Well, it won't be the first time he's tried to woo me into medicine."

Jess hadn't moved from his side, her hand still resting lightly on his good arm. "You should sit down."

"I'm fine, really," he protested, but allowed her to guide him to a chair anyway.

Colton looked up, his eyes serious. "Does it hurt a lot?"

"Not too bad," Carson lied smoothly. "Your mom's worried about nothing."

"I saw blood," Colton's tone was low, hints of fear from the earlier incident still laced his words.

"Just a scratch," Carson assured him. "And look—I got a cool bandage out of it." He flexed his arm slightly, immediately regretting the movement when pain shot through his shoulder.

Forehead folded, Colton didn't seem convinced, but Brady nudged his hand, demanding more attention.

Alice bustled in from the kitchen, carrying a loaf of fresh bread. "When grandmothers have nothing but time to worry, they bake. There are four more loaves where this came from."

"Good. Apparently getting kicked by a horse makes a man hungry." Carson flashed his mother a smile, doing his best to make today seem like no big deal.

"You're not the only one," Preston spoke up.

"Hear, hear," multiple voices echoed.

"All right." Alice glared at every adult in the room. "Point taken. Everyone to the dining room."

Slowly, they all filed into the dining room, shuffling around, taking their seats, comments back and forth about the wild horses. Garret teasing that Carson probably scared the mare more than the mare scared him.

"Who said the mare scared me?" Colton eased into his chair. Jess sat at his side.

Garret raised one brow at him, calling his brother's bluff. "You're just lucky none of the other horses came after you. The last thing anyone wants to do is tangle with a miffed stallion."

"Amen to that," Preston poured a glass of water for his wife, then himself.

"The important thing," his mom placed a tray of lasagna on the table, "is that no one was seriously hurt."

Nodding at his mother, Carson noticed Colton seemed awfully quiet, his movements slow, hesitant. Once the adrenaline had dissipated, even he had been left a bit on edge, he couldn't imagine Colton was any different. What he didn't know, was how to help his son put the incident behind him without repercussions.

As he considered options and the situation, Colton chuckled and Carson took a second look. Brady had settled under the table at Colton's feet, licking his fingers, and sneakily begging for scraps. Carson should have known that Brady would be the best therapist, he'd done so much to help Samson adjust, and even though Colton wasn't a K-9, Brady was doing what Brady did best.

Seated beside Carson, Jess's knee briefly touched his under the table. Her cheeks pinkened a moment and he couldn't help but smile. There wasn't anything about this woman, anything she did, that he didn't love.

His mother's voice, saying grace, thanking God for keeping them safe and bringing them all home together, interrupted his thoughts. Carson found himself adding his own silent thanks. Not just for the safe outcome, but for all the blessings bestowed on him recently—two in particular.

"Was it me," Carson sank into the recliner, "or was that the best lasagna you've ever made?"

A smile split his mom's face. "Charmer."

Jess couldn't help but chuckle at the family dynamic. After a miserably harrowing and nerve-wracking day, here they all were, relaxed, calm, and teasing each other no less. Love filled the room from floor to ceiling.

Cards fanned out in front of his face, his eyes narrowed in concentration, even Colton seemed to have lost his nervous jitters. Since dinner began he'd settled considerably, the tension gradually leaving his small shoulders as the meal progressed. Now, locked in an intense game of Go Fish with Garret, he seemed almost back to his normal self. "Got any threes?" Colton eyed his uncle suspiciously.

"Go fish," Garret winked.

When Colton reached for the deck, Jess checked her watch. "Getting late, sweetie. Better wrap this up soon."

"But Mom," Colton whined as only a nine-year-old could.

"Not till after our game," Garret countered, ruffling his nephew's hair. "Can't leave a man hanging when he's on a winning streak."

From across the room, Alice smiled over her coffee cup. "I'll take him up when they're done, Jess. You've had a long day."

Wasn't that the understatement of the year? What must have been only minutes out by the canyon had felt like hours at the time. She truly was drained.

Balancing a mug of coffee with his good arm, Carson slipped through the back door. Without a word, she followed him out onto the porch.

The evening had cooled, the Texas heat giving way to a quiet night. Stars were sparkling in the darkened sky, pinpricks of light against a blackened backdrop. Carson stood at the railing, his back to her, shoulders slightly hunched.

"Nights never looked anything like this in Dallas." She came to stand at his side.

"Light pollution."

Her head bobbed. So much was in her mind and heart, she had no idea where to begin. "You lied to Colton. My money's on that arm hurts a lot more than 'not too bad,' doesn't it?"

Carson's mouth quirked into a half-smile. "Maybe a little."

"Hm, maybe, huh?"

He shrugged his good shoulder. "Worth it."

The simple statement hung between them in the evening air. Worth it. Two small words that somehow contained everything.

"I don't know what I would have done if anything had happened to Colton."

Carson swallowed hard then nodded.

"Or you," she said softly.

His gaze turned from the distant horizon to her. Their eyes met, and something shifted inside her. Could she tell him all that she'd been feeling since coming to the ranch? What she understood now better than ever before?

"Jess," he set his coffee mug on the railing, turning to face her fully. "We need to talk."

Her heart stuttered in her chest. No good ever came from a conversation that started with, we need to talk. "Okay."

"First, I want to thank you."

Thank her? "You're welcome, but for what?"

Tipping his head to one side, a slight smile teased at one corner of his mouth. "For being the same person I remember from so long ago, for coming all the way out here in person to tell me about Colton, for agreeing to this hare-brained idea of a marrying to save the ranch, for letting me become a father to Colton," he hesitated a second, "I could go on, but that's a good start."

"Well," she tried not to let her nerves show, "If I'm anything at all like I was before Colton was born, that's because of you." She waved her arm toward the house. "And everyone here. You've all been wonderful. It's the first home I've had in such a long time."

That hint of a smile blossomed. "I'm sorry you've had it rough for so long. I, I wish I'd fought harder."

Now she cocked her head to one side. "I don't understand."

Moving forward slightly, he reached for her hand with his good arm, then must have thought better of it, dropping his hand to his side. "The first time I saw you walking across the quadrangle, you had my attention. When you walked into the same class as me, I was hooked. Then, as time went by and we became friends, you had my heart."

She knew she was staring wide-eyed at him, but, was he saying what she thought she was saying.

"I had no choice but to bite my tongue and keep my feelings to myself. You were dating Todd, you seemed happy."

Her mouth opened slightly to speak, but Carson held his palm open at her.

"Please. Let me finish or I'll never get it all out."

Biting down on her lower lip, she nodded.

"When Todd walked out on you that night at the frat party, when you seemed so angry at him, so sure you were through with him forever, I'd never been happier in my life."

Unable to speak, she just listened.

"Yes, we had a few drinks, and yes my wisdom filter was shot, but if you didn't know it then, I'll tell you, now. For me it wasn't just a one night stand, I showed you everything I felt inside in the best way I knew how."

That brought a smile to her face. Perhaps it wasn't the appropriate response, but she'd finally recognized that night that her feelings for Carson had gone far past mere friendship.

"I savored every minute we spent together for the next few weeks," He raked his hand through his hair. "I had dreams. Hopes. Plans."

"Oh, Carson," the words slipped out.

"I know we made a deal."

Again, she nodded.

"But I don't think I can go through with it." His eyes closed and he heaved a deep sigh. "I'm in love with you, Jess. I always have been. I just can't continue this pretense. If I do, I won't be able to watch you leave me. Not again."

Tears built up in her eyes. Frantically trying to blink them back, she reached for his hand, the one he'd pulled away moments ago. "That night, I learned something too. I learned that until you laughed with me, sat with me, held me, I didn't have a clue what love was. When you spent the next few weeks, building a new relationship level, I learned what it was like to be cherished, respected, and loved. And I discovered that I'd fallen in love with my best friend."

Carson's mouth dropped slightly open then snapped shut as he swallowed hard. "I can only pray that somewhere in your heart, enough of that love is still there that I can win you over once again."

This time she actually chuckled. "Silly man. You don't have to win anything. I know now. I've never stopped loving you."

To her surprise, Carson pulled a small velvet box from his pocket. "The week before you left, I bought this. I've been carrying it around since you agreed to our deal, but it didn't feel right for a charade. In college I didn't have a lot of money. I know it's not much, but I couldn't bring myself to sell it or give it away. I guess you could say, no matter how hard I tried to move on, I couldn't let go of my only connection to you and what we had." Suddenly, he dropped to one knee, the closed box still in his hand. "Jess, I love you today more than yesterday, and I know that love will continue to grow if you'll give me the chance. Will you be my wife, my life partner, for real?"

She had no idea what the proper protocol was for the happiest moment of your life, but before he could open the box, she dropped to her knees and threw her arms around his neck. "It's perfect. I love you. Yes, yes, and yes."

Laughter in his voice, he wrapped his good arm around her waist. "But you haven't seen it yet."

"It doesn't matter." She kissed his lips and pulled back. "It's perfect. You're perfect."

"We're perfect," he corrected.

Peace filling her for the first time in too long, she smiled even wider. "Yeah, we are."

EPILOGUE

"**I** just love parades." Alice Sweet stood at her grandson's side.

Cotton candy in hand, Colton grinned up at his Nonnie, "Me too."

Ever since that terrifying moment with Colton and the wild mare, things had shifted at the Sweet Ranch. Garret wasn't a man of the world by any means, but even he could feel the difference. They were all truly a family. Heck, Colton had come barreling down the stairs one day, a new picture of Brady in his hand, calling at the top of his lungs for *Dad*. Garret thought for sure Carson was going to break down and cry in front of the kid.

"Do you see them?" Alice scanned over the tops of the crowd.

"Do I see who?" Garret followed his mother's gaze even though he didn't have a clue who he was looking for.

"Carson and Jess. They're helping Aunt Liz and Vicki with some last-minute decorations on their float and are supposed to meet up with us, but I don't see them yet and the floats are starting down Main Street.

Well, his mother was right about that much, the first float covered in enough crepe paper to cover the whole town, had begun lumbering down the street.

"Look, Nonnie. It's purple."

"Yes, it is dear."

Apparently, talking on the colors of Mardis Gras, even though National Corn Hole day had nothing to do with Mardis Gras, the new quilt shop in town was tossing purple and gold colored beads from their float and the spectators were loving it.

Garret shifted his weight, scanning the crowd again.

"There they are!" Colton pointed excitedly, jumping up and down for a better view.

Garret followed his nephew's finger and spotted Carson and Jess, every few seconds glancing at each other and smiling, making their way through the crowd. From what he could see, there were now two happy couples in the Sweet family. He had no clue how his brothers had gotten so lucky as to strike a match of convenience, and wind up so deeply in love. For years, Garret doubted anyone could be as happy as his mom and dad had been, and yet, first Preston and now Carson, had proved him wrong.

They moved in sync, Carson's hand resting lightly at the small of Jess's back, guiding her through the throng. When someone jostled them, Carson pulled her closer, and the beaming smile she gave him in return was like a secret language only they understood.

"Sorry we're late," Carson eased closer to his son. "Aunt Vicki and Liz had words over Mildred McEntire wearing all the bling on their float."

"Carson refereed beautifully," Jess chuckled, reaching out to brush a strand of wayward tinsel from Carson's shoulder.

Garret noted how his brother leaned into the touch, how his eyes followed Jess even as he ruffled Colton's hair in greeting. There was no sign of the cautious, calculating businessman Carson had been just months ago. This was a man transformed.

"You've got a little…" Carson gestured to the corner of Jess's mouth where a smudge of glitter sparkled.

Before she could react, he brushed it away with his thumb, his touch lingering longer than necessary. Jess blushed, and Garret had to look away, feeling like a voyeur, even if they were standing smack dab in the middle of Main Street. His gaze drifted to Preston and Sarah who had arrived late and squeezed in on his mom's other side. Another couple who spoke silently with their eyes. At least he wouldn't have to worry about his sisters. Rachel would be on Jillian's float and neither would be making lovey-dovey eyes at anyone but the crowd.

"The Corn Hole Heaven float is coming!" Colton tugged at Carson's sleeve, breaking the spell.

Sure enough, Aunt Liz and Vicki's elaborate creation approached—a massive corn hole board decorated with thousands of sequins, crowned by none other than Mildred McEntire in a tiara that could rival the one given to Miss Universe. The family erupted in cheers.

"It's something, isn't it?" Carson grinned, slipping his arm around Jess's waist.

"Only in Honeysuckle," she leaned into him.

As Mildred waved regally from her perch, tossing handfuls of corn kernels dipped in silver paint, Garret found himself watching his brother instead of the parade. Carson pointed out details of the float to Colton, who now sat contentedly on his shoulders for a better view. Jess stood beside them, her hand resting on Carson's arm, her face tilted up to them both with such open affection that Garret felt a tug in his chest. They made it look so blasted easy.

When had his pragmatic, business-minded brother become this man who gazed at his wife like she hung the moon? The man who hoisted a nine-year-old onto his shoulders without a second thought, who threw back his head and laughed at something Jess whispered in his ear?

And Jess—the nervous city girl who'd arrived at their ranch just months ago—now stood with the easy confidence of someone who knew exactly where she belonged. She caught Garret watching and flashed him a warm smile, without a word, including him in their happiness.

Maybe that was what struck him most. The way they'd built something that somehow made room for all of them. Not just Carson, Jess, and Colton, but the entire Sweet family. Even him, with all his edges and silences.

"Earth to Garret." His mom nudged him. "Do you want some lemonade?"

He blinked, realizing he'd missed part of the conversation. "Sure, thanks."

As his mother wandered off toward the lemonade stand, Garret found himself standing next to Carson. "This may be the best parade turnout yet."

Carson nodded, his gaze darting from the parade to his wife, and then he glanced up to grin at his son. "Yep. All is good. Very good."

There was so much contentment in those simple words that Garret wondered if there was some kind of magic attached to the family trust. Or maybe it was just wishful thinking. After all, with Jillian and Rachel still struggling to find believable future mates willing to give up a year of their lives for little reward, he seemed to be top on the list of who needed to marry next. Like he'd once heard the hero of some romcom say, he believed in marriage too much to marry just anybody. That was clearly going to have to change, but wouldn't it be something if maybe, just maybe, the trust had a little more magic to offer?

Enjoy an excerpt from
Sweet Temptation

Checking his watch, Garret shoved the kitchen door open. Lingering scents of roast beef and fresh biscuits told him he wasn't too late for dinner. The familiar sounds of his family drifted from the dining room—Mason's excited chatter, Carson's measured responses, his sister Jillian's gentle laughter, and of course his mother directing the evening. After a day of corralling seventh graders through the complexities of American history, followed by two hours of mending the fence line, all he wanted was food and his bed, in that order.

"There he is." His mom grinned up at him. "A little longer and I was going to send Brady to go find you."

The retired military dog, lounging at Mason's feet, barely lifted his head at the mention of his name.

"Sorry." Garret slid into his seat between Rachel and Preston. "I had a meeting after school with some parents that ran long and I'd told Clint that I would take care of the break in the fence by the east line that needed attention."

Rachel passed him the mashed potatoes. "You look dead on your feet."

"Says the woman who works day and night to save the world." Serving spoon in hand, he loaded his plate.

"To another day of the Sweet siblings burning the candle at both ends." Seated across from them, Jillian raised her water glass. "No pun intended."

That made just about everyone at the table chuckle. Jillian's candle shop, Heaven Scent, had become one of the most popular shops on Main Street.

Garret dug into his food, the home cooked meal a major

step up from the sandwich he'd hastily swallowed hours ago between classes. At the head of the table, despite the financial tightrope everyone walked, his mother beamed at her assembled family. Preston and Carson's recent marriages had done a lot to ease some of the pressure, but there was still a long way to go. Since his sisters were having a hard time finding temporary spouses, and Kade was serving in the military overseas, the short straw, so to speak, fell to Garret. He needed to find a reasonable woman willing to play house with him—in name only of course—sooner than later.

"Any sign of the horses?" Her plate empty, his mother dabbed at the corner of her mouth with the napkin. "Clint is wondering if maybe it's not the cattle, but the horses knocking down the fences."

"Could be." Preston nodded. "It would certainly explain why it's only become a problem recently."

The idea of the problem being wild horses and not decrepit fence posts sat much better with Garret. Especially since the ranch was still bleeding red ink. Big time.

"Your father would have loved having wild horses on the ranch." His mom chuckled to herself. "Well, until they tore down the first fence."

Again, the family around the table laughed with their mother. Chatter continued through dessert. Mason had grown restless and excused himself from the table, Brady faithfully following him. Until Mason arrived, Brady was their mother's keeper, but not anymore.

Pushing away from the table, Carson stood and came around to Garret's seat. "I'm heading upstairs to make sure Mason's getting started on his homework." He glanced up, waiting for his mom to carry her dishes into the kitchen, then leaned over, speaking softly. "Family meeting in Dad's study."

Garret nodded. That could only mean one thing. A financial update, or heaven forbid, a new problem.

"Nonnie." Jess came off the bottom step and swung around into the kitchen.

His mom had already popped her head out. "You rang?"

"You're being paged. Mason's didn't have much homework. Now he wants Nonnie to read him a story, or ten, before bed."

Smiling wider than the Cheshire Cat, their mom tossed the dishrag aside and hurried out of the kitchen and up the stairs.

One by one, the siblings and their spouses each filed into the study. The habit of gathering here to discuss the ranch happenings had become second nature.

"So, what's the story?" Jillian asked.

"Morning Glory," Rachel sang.

"What's the word," Sarah Sue chimed in.

To Garret's surprise, all three giggling, sang—loudly, "Hummingbird."

The three brothers looked to each other and then to the women now laughing like a couple of school girls.

"What's the deal?" Preston asked from his seat at the desk.

"Don't you remember *Bye Bye Birdie*?" Rachel looked at him as if he'd forgotten his own birthday.

All three men shook their heads.

"How could you?" Jillian shook her head. "We only watched the movie about a hundred times over the years. You used to love the scene with Ann Margaret dancing."

Garret had to smile. His mother loved old movies and usually insisted her children suffer through them, but he had developed a bit of a crush on Ann Margaret from an early age. Still, whatever his sisters had just sung didn't ring any bells.

"Never mind." Sarah Sue sighed, her gaze directed at her husband. "Care to update?"

"The good news is the bank has stopped threatening to foreclose." Preston scrolled through something on the computer screen. "The bad news is we're still in the hole up to our necks and funds are stretched really thin."

"Darn shame the hay baler disappeared before we could sell it." Jess leaned against her husband.

Jillian nodded. "That would have helped raise some fast cash."

"Any new clues about who took it?" Rachel interjected.

"Nope." Preston swung his head left then right. "But the cameras haven't picked up any new strange activity, so there is that."

"I'll take any good news." Rachel leaned back in her seat, her one leg dangling over the arm of the chair, swinging like a pendulum.

"Then you won't want to hear this." Preston pulled a few pieces of paper from the printer. "This is our current financial picture. At the bottom you'll see what we still owe, what we're scheduled to pay at the end of the month, and how much we're short."

Garret let out a slow whistle. The numbers added up to more than he'd expected. The problem—and answer—were clear. They needed more money—a lot of it—and he needed to find someone soon to pass for his wife or things were going to go south fast. Very fast.

"You've completely lost your mind."

"I have not." Jackie Drake grabbed another shirt from the drawer and shoved it into the suitcase. "Once Brad understands that I'm willing to give up everything for him, that he doesn't have to ask me to leave behind my friends and home, he'll be over the moon."

"Hmm." Katie, her dearest friend since their sophomore year of college, pretty much thought Jackie should be committed. Of course, she'd never liked Brad. "Maybe you should just go for a short visit? See what it's like. If it doesn't work out, you can come home."

"Too late." She rolled another blouse. "Yesterday was my last day at work."

"What?" Katie's eyes almost fell out of her head. "You quit a job you love?"

"Gave my notice two weeks ago." Her favorite slippers went into the bag next.

"And you didn't tell me?"

Pausing, Jackie leveled her gaze with her bestie. "No, because you would have tried to talk me out of it."

"Damn right I would have." Katie glanced around the one bedroom apartment. "And this place?"

"I won't need it."

"You gave this up too?"

Jackie nodded. "Had to pay off the lease, but it's worth it."

Holding up both her hands, palms out, Katie shook her head and huffed like a bull about to charge. "And how much did that cost you?"

"Only three months rent." She tried to make it sound like she hadn't had to clean out all her bank accounts to pay for the move.

"*Only.*" Her bestie dropped her forehead into her hand and rubbed it very slowly before looking up again. "Jack, you know I want you to be happy."

"I will be. Brad's perfect."

"For what? The man is a poster boy for the modern playboy. He cheated on you more times than I can count."

"They were just distractions."

"Distractions? Are you listening to yourself? He cheated on you. Breaking dates without calling is his MO. Not to mention he's made it perfectly clear he doesn't want children."

Holding a lightweight sweater, she froze mid motion. "That's only because he hasn't been around them enough. I'm sure once we're married, he'll change his mind."

"For the smartest woman I know," Katie fisted her hands on her hips, "you sure become a blithering idiot when it comes to Brad."

"Gee, thanks."

"Seriously. I want you to be happy, but with a nice guy who appreciates and cherishes you and wants to settle down and have a family. It's not like you're pushing forty or something. What's the hurry?"

"I'm not twenty any more either. If I want to have the big family I've always dreamed of, Brad is my best option."

Katie sighed. "I'm not going to talk you out of this, am I?"

Shaking her head, she closed her suitcase. "Nope. And this is about it. What I don't wear anymore has either been dropped off at the consignment store or donated. I've already sold most of the kitchen things, and I have a few people coming by later today for some more of the furniture and odds and ends. What isn't gone by the time I leave tomorrow is going to be picked up by a local shelter."

"Lord love a duck." Katie rolled her eyes. "Jackie, please. Use your common sense. What are you going to do when you reach West Texas? Buy everything new with money you don't have?"

"I won't need anything. Brad's apartment was way nicer than this place, I'm sure wherever he's living in Millers Creek will be just as nice."

"Millers Creek. Sounds like a brewery. I don't like this—any of it."

"I know." Setting the bag down by the side of the bed, she smiled at her friend. "I appreciate how much you worry about me, but I'm okay. This will be good."

"Didn't your mother ever teach you there are plenty of fish in the sea? Why do you insist on hanging onto this slick eel of a guy?"

"He is not slick."

Katie merely raised a brow at her and sighed.

"He's charming, good looking, well educated, well employed, and we know we'll be perfectly happy together."

"We? Brad actually said this to you?" Katie crossed her arms.

"Well," she glanced down at the bag she'd just packed, "not in those words."

"Uh huh." Letting her arms fall to her side, Katie inched closer to her friend. "Please, tell me you at least have a back up plan if Brad doesn't work out."

She shook her head and grinned with a little more self assurance than she felt. "Won't need one."

What she needed now was to fly to Midland tomorrow,

then drive to Millers Creek, and then, she'd be reunited with Brad. So what if he had no idea she was coming? Doesn't everybody love surprises?

Read more of Sweet Temptation available now

MEET CHRIS

USA TODAY Bestselling Author of dozens of contemporary novels, including the award winning Aloha Series, Chris Keniston lives in suburban Dallas with her husband, two human children, and two canine children. Though she loves her puppies equally, she admits being especially attached to her German Shepherd rescue. After all, even dogs deserve a happily ever after.

More on Chris and all her books can be found at
www.chriskeniston.com

Follow Chris' Monday Blog at her website
ChrisKenistonAuthor

Follow Chris on Facebook at
ChrisKenistonAuthor

Never miss a New Release!
Sign up for News from Chris:
www.chriskeniston.com/newsletter.html

Questions? Comments?
I would love to hear from you! You can reach me at:
chris@chriskeniston.com

www.ingramcontent.com/pod-product-compliance
Lightning Source LLC
Chambersburg PA
CBHW031517010826
48973CB00013B/2681